Not
Another
Bard's Tale

Not Another Bard's Tale

JEAN DAVIS

All characters, places and events portrayed in this novel are fictional. No resemblance to any specific person, place or event is intended.

Not Another Bard's Tale

www.jeandavisauthor.com

ISBN-13:   (print) 978-1-7345701-8-2
                (ebook) 978-1-7345701-9-9

First Edition: April 2021

Published by StreamlineDesign LLC

Also by Jean Davis

The Last God
Sahmara
A Broken Race
Destiny Pills and Space Wizards
Dreams Of Stars and Lies

The Narvan
Trust
Chain of Gray
Bound In Blue

❦ 1 ❦

Bruce's Best Spent Coin

Bruce glanced toward the docks where several ships were moored, their masts bobbing madly as a sudden rush of heavy wind buffeted the sea-side market. Horse-drawn carts raced by and shouting came from the next street over. He gripped the rough wood of the stall and squinted against the blowing dirt to read the poorly painted sign: Holden's famous Herman! The great seer of the West!

A hunched man in a faded blue robe adorned with what may have been golden stars and moons bared his scant teeth. "I see an auspicious future for you, knight." He held out an age-spotted hand. "But the details require payment."

His past hadn't been all too profitable and presently Bruce was in a state he preferred to call 'between quests'. If a single coin could give him a push in a better direction it would be well spent. He dug into the coin purse he wore under his armor. He placed a chipped copper disc with a hole in the middle onto the seer's palm. "That's one of my last. You better tell me something worthwhile."

"You listen to old Herman now, my visions always be true."

People hurried past, glancing over their shoulders. "Get on with it then. The day's almost done and I need to find the inn."

Herman cleared his throat with a great hacking cough, followed by a hesitant wheeze and another cough, slightly less phlegm-filled than the last. "Show me your palm."

Bruce held out his hand, wondering what the old man hoped to see in the fading light. He probably had his prophetic line of mysterious words already on his tongue; the palm was all for show. He scowled, already wishing he'd spent his coin on dinner or a pint of ale.

"All right then." Herman traced the lines on his palm with thin, wrinkled fingers. "What you seek lies at the Wall of Nok. You must travel far and the way will not be easy."

A shadow passed overhead, like a brief sampling of nightfall, but then it was gone. Something crashed at the other end of the marketplace. The ground shook. Screams filled the air.

What a load of dung. Bruce yanked his hand away. The evening air grew warm, almost unbearably so within his armor.

The shaking of the ground became more intense. The wooden stalls creaked. A host of people ran by. Shopkeepers watched them. Several abandoned their wares and joined the running crowd. Herman eyed the coin with determination as it bounced about on the quaking counter of the stall.

Bruce made a grab for his coin.

The surprisingly spry seer snatched it up. "When you reach the wall, you will find—"

A giant, brown-scaled head atop a long neck lined with tall spikes loomed over the booth. Two great golden eyes surveyed Bruce and then locked on to the old man. The dragon's jaws gaped open to reveal two wicked rows of teeth.

Bruce screamed like a little girl.

The dragon snatched up the seer and chewed with what appeared to be great satisfaction. It swallowed and then picked at one of his dagger-length teeth with a claw. The copper coin fell onto the counter.

The dragon's rancid, hot breath blasted over Bruce. "You wouldn't happen to know where the nearest lake is, do you? I always find mystics a bit dry."

Bruce pointed to the far end of town with a shaking hand.

"Thank you." The dragon flapped its wings, knocking flat the booth and all of those surrounding it, sending the goods flying in all directions.

As the dragon lifted into the sky Bruce's reflexes finally kicked in. He drew his sword. Another rush of people, scattered in their efforts to pick a direction in which to flee, flooded through the decimated market.

A short young man stopped, gazing up at the dragon and then following its line of ascent to Bruce and his sword. "You scared the dragon off! You saved us all!"

"I don't know about..." Bruce glanced at the sword in his hand. If he meant to change his fortune, he was going to have to up his advertising game. "Yes. Yes, I did. Fearsome beast, but no match for a knight like me."

"Behold, our savior!" the man called to all who passed by. A crowd gathered around. Cheers filled the air. The man drew closer. "Tell us, oh brave knight, what is your name that we might remember your great deed this day?"

Bruce's chest swelled within his dented armor and a smile split his face in half. His steady voice bellowed, "Bruce Gawain." He sheathed his sword and placed his hands upon his hips in a pose he'd practiced many times, knowing it showed off his manly form and gave him an aura of victory.

The young man grinned. "Well met, Bruce Gawain. You must be hungry after your fight with the dragon. Come, let us celebrate. My cousin owns an inn. I'm sure he would be honored to give you a room and a fine meal."

"Why, thank you. That would be most welcome." Bruce swaggered after his eager admirer.

The fortune telling may have been a bust, but it sure seemed as if his luck had changed for the better. "Thanks, Herman. Your sacrifice is most appreciated," he said under his breath.

The crowd followed them out of the market and down the main street to a two-story building with a sign sporting a smiling sheep. Loud laughter spilled out the open door. The man waved him along as they made their way through the rowdy, drinking throng. He drew to a stop next to the long wooden bar and jerked a finger at a blonde woman behind the counter.

"That's my cousin's daughter, Olga." He winked at Bruce. "What do you think?"

Her billowy white blouse did little to hide her thick arms and strong jaw. However, when she slid a mug of frothy ale down the bar, her ample breasts affirmed that she was indeed a woman. Her big blue eyes looked him over. She addressed the young man. "Who is this?"

"A knight, a hero. He saved the marketplace from an attack by a dragon just now. You should have seen it, Olga. All he had to do was brandish his mighty sword and the dragon fled."

"Is that so? I could have done that." She turned her attention to Bruce. "I'm pretty handy with a sword myself."

"Is that so?" Bruce eyed an empty mug in her hand. "Fighting dragons makes me thirsty."

She set the mug down. "Doesn't sound like much of a fight to me. Sounds more like you waving your sword around. The dragon probably caught a glint of light in its eye and that scared it off."

Bruce frowned. How dare she diminish his performance in front of his adoring fan. "No, I assure you, it was my skill with the sword."

The cousin clapped Bruce on his metal-encased shoulder. "Come on, Olga, I promised Bruce a drink and dinner. I'm sure your father would agree that having such a hero under his roof is an honor."

"Don't forget the free night's lodging." Bruce offered Olga his most charming smile.

She set down the towel she'd been using to clean the counter, and thrust her hands onto her hips in a manner that did everything to accentuate her broad form. He couldn't believe she'd stolen his move. Just who did this large barmaid think she was?

Olga leaned over the counter, giving him a deadpan stare. "If you are such a great knight, how about you show us some of your skill. You know, for those of us who missed it earlier. Then I'll see to that meal and a bed."

"I've already defeated a dragon today," said Bruce."Doesn't that at least get me a drink?"

She looked to those that had entered with him. "Did anyone see this glorious battle?"

Bruce looked to his admirer.

The cousin shrugged. "I saw the dragon fly off and Bruce there with his sword. What more do I need to see?"

Olga poured half a mug and set it down with a heavy *thunk* in front of Bruce. "I need to see some proof before I give anything else away for free. Drink up, and then I'll meet you out back."

Two women in the crowd that had followed from the market draped themselves over each of his shoulders. "We'd love to see you in action."

He quaffed the bitter, watery drink and wondered just what he was in for with the buxom, yet bulky bar wench. She seemed to be giving him mixed signals. Not that he was opposed to her more enticing charms, but the other two women were pretty clear with what they were offering and they seemed like a far easier choice.

Thanks to Olga, everyone around him now expected a grand performance. Bruce sighed inwardly. Why couldn't anything simply be easy?

With his loosely-termed ale finished, Bruce stood, determined to make the best of the situation Olga had created. She might be large, but she probably moved like an ox. Why would a barmaid have any skill with a sword anyway?

"Let's be at it then, my stomach could use a good meal," he said.

Olga waved at another woman dressed in a

similar low-cut shirt, but this barmaid was thin and curvy in all the right places. "This is my sister Svetlana."

The beauty flashed him a dimpled smile. "Go easy on him Olga, he's a handsome one."

"You say that about every man who walks in here with a sword, claiming to be a knight." Olga shoved her sister behind the bar. "Take care of things while I'm out back."

The pretty woman nodded, her blond curls bobbing.

Olga looked Bruce up and down. "I shouldn't be long."

Mutters rolled through the crowd. Bets started to change hands. Sweat began to gather under Bruce's armor. Whispers and footsteps followed them out into the back alley. The onlookers gathered at one end, giving Olga and Bruce room to fight at the other.

Bruce unsheathed his sword. "So, what exactly are we doing here? I don't want to hurt you."

"I'd worry more about me hurting you."

"You don't even have any armor."

"Hard to do any real work in armor. But you wouldn't know anything about that, would you, *knight*?"

Olga took an offered sword from the crowd and approached Bruce with a gleam in her eye. Her skirts swished with each step forward. She slashed at him with all the force of a hardened swordsman.

He scrambled to block her, his wrist reverberating with the power behind her blow. Realizing she meant business, he tried to stop watching her chest bounce with each thrust and concentrate more on making himself look less inept. It wasn't so much that he was inept as much as distracted. He swore she tugged her blouse a bit lower just to taunt him.

"They've grown lax with handing out the title of knight. You have yet to impress me. As a matter of fact, I bet even Svetlana could hold you off." Her chest barely heaved and her voice was as steady as it had been inside.

As they fought, his sweat began to form rivulets, making his armor quite uncomfortable. His hair grew wet, plastering itself to his face in a most unflattering manner.

Bruce blocked another of her powerful blows. Fighting with her more womanly sister sounded pretty good at the moment. The crowd cheered. He was disheartened to realize that they called out her name rather than his. Had his great dragon victory already faded from their minds?

The sword in his hand reminded him of the war, the only one he'd fought in. Holden was much too peaceful of a country for his liking. Men grunting, swords clanging, and the smell of death heavy in the air. Here, there was horse dung, the rattle of carts on the cobbles, and men and women cheering for his opponent. This was all wrong. Swordfights weren't for bets, for fun and entertainment. Swords were for settling disputes, defending honor, and protecting one's country from enemies. And women, large busty women—even those who otherwise much resembled men—had no business carrying a sword. Feeling anger rise in his blood, he slashed at her, knocking her blade aside for the first time. And then a second and third time.

Ground slowly became his. Olga backed toward the crowd, blocking and swinging but with less luck than before.

Luck, yes, that must be what she had. And perhaps a talent for distraction. Any woman as large as this one would have to have some sort of talent to find a man. Not that he imagined any man would take a swordswoman of any degree as a wife. No wonder she was so aggressive. The poor thing must be lonely, thriving on the adulation of the crowd when she could get it.

Their swords met with a loud clang, both of them pressing against one another, vying for control of the now crowded, torch-lit alley. Olga's footing slipped. She slid backward, allowing Bruce to press harder. Her sword scraped against his armor. She bent to keep his blade away from her glistening bare flesh.

She sighed and brought her sword down. The crowd went silent.

"All right, fine, you win," she said.

Bruce expected a rush of adulation upon his

victory but got little more of a half-hearted pat on the back. Men muttered as coins changed hands and the crowd dispersed.

"What do you want for dinner?" Olga asked.

Bruce shrugged, the disappointment of the crowd's response and their rapid dissipation dissolved his enthusiasm. "Food."

"Yes, I got that. What kind?"

"The kind you eat."

Olga's brows drew together. "No kidding. What kind do you want to eat?"

"The good kind."

"That would be stew. Svetlana makes a great mutton stew."

Bruce's stomach rumbled. He followed her back inside the inn and took a seat at the bar. Olga returned the sword to the man who had donated it and resumed her post behind the bar. She nodded to Svetlana. The pretty sister slid a heel of bread along with a steaming bowl of stew in front of him. That was followed by a full mug of ale and a wink that almost made him forget the lackluster response to his victory out back.

"Don't worry, this is the good stuff," she flashed him her dimpled smile and twirled a curl on her finger. "So, where are you from?"

"East of Holden, down by the cliffs overlooking the sea."

"Wow, that sounds far away."

"It is." He puffed out his chest. "I've traveled far."

She nodded. "You must be tired."

"I am." He took a big bite of the stew filled with hearty chunks of turnips and carrots and actual identifiable pieces of meat in rich brown sauce. "This is very good. Olga was right."

Svetlana blushed. "Oh, thank you."

"With such thick woodland surrounding your town, where do you find pasture for the sheep?"

"Pasture? Oh, no. We don't have to worry about that."

"Why ever not? How else do you feed your sheep?"

"Olga didn't tell you?"

Bruce put his heel of bread down. "Tell me what?"

Svetlana twirled around, raising her hands to the roof. "I was chosen by the sheep god when I was a little girl. He came to me when I was lost. I'd been playing outside and had wandered far from home. We had a long talk, and then he led me back to town."

Sheep god? Bruce fought to keep from laughing out loud. Surely, there was no such thing. "And what did you talk about?"

Her face scrunched up and she pursed her lips for a long moment. "Everyone asks that, but I can't remember. He was nice though, and soft. He had a thick woolen coat. It kept me warm all the way back to the edge of town.

"And what does that have to do with why you don't have to feed your sheep?"

"Well, every night, I go to bed."

"Don't we all?" Bruce shook his head and took another bite of stew.

"Every morning, I wake up and a sheep is there, sleeping next to me."

Stew shot up Bruce's nose as he laughed and then choked.

Svetlana pouted. "It's not nice to make fun of the chosen one." She crossed her arms over her chest. "Thanks to me, our inn never runs out of mutton."

He cleared the stew from his nostrils and took a long pull from his mug. "And what is your end of this deal with this sheep god?"

She leaned in close and whispered, "as long as I remain a virgin, my family will never go hungry."

"Just as well. I can't imagine any man would enjoy waking up with a sheep in his bed along with his wife."

Svetlana looked forlorn. "My father sent Olga away to be trained as a swordswoman to protect me when he couldn't be around. He's often gone on business."

That explained a few things. He gave Olga a wary glance. Finding her busy serving other patrons far from him and her charge, he returned his attention to Svetlana.

"What does your father do?"

"We own a chain of inns throughout Holden. Sheep's Inn, I'm sure you've heard of us. We're quite popular with the travelers."

"No, sorry."

"How about our slogan? You can count on us?"

"Nope, sorry."

Svetlana sighed. "I'll have to talk to father about that. Our marketing needs work, I guess. Give me a minute and I'll get a room ready for you upstairs."

He watched the gentle sway of her ascent up the stairs. Only once she was out of sight did he finish his meal. When he slid the bowl away, he found the admirer from the market back by his side.

"So, where are you off to next? Where's the next big adventure? Are you chasing the dragon?"

Bruce shifted his scabbard and turned around to take in the denizens of the room. He adopted his clearest and deepest voice. "I travel to the Wall of Nok."

The young man stopped mid-sip. "Did you say the Wall of Nok?"

Bruce smiled wide, making sure to get all his bright white teeth in view for maximum effect. "I did. Do you know of it?"

"I heard tell that the Wall lies beyond the Forest of Fear and the Desert of Despair."

Bruce almost laughed out loud but caught himself before his dear admirer took offense. "I've traveled all through Holden and not heard of these places. Surely, you jest. I mean, why not toss in the Caves of Doom, while you're at it."

"No. That doesn't work at all. The place and word must start with the same letter. I thought they taught this stuff at knight school." He shook his head. "Besides, everyone knows the Caves of Cacophony are in Bellshore. That's the total opposite direction of where you have to go. The Wall of Nok is in Gambreland, across the Sea of Sickness."

"What are you, a walking, talking map?"

The young man harrumphed, got up from his stool, and stomped off.

Damn. Admirers were hard to come by and he'd managed to tick off the first one he'd had in weeks. Bruce pounded his mug on the counter until Olga filled it for him. He took a drink. She'd given him the bitter, watered-down stuff again. He grimaced and made a note to only pound his mug when Svetlana was around. He swished the swill around in his mouth.

Leaving the borders of Holden set his nerves on edge. He'd never been out of the country. What language did they speak in Gambreland? He didn't even know. And a boat? He didn't have enough coin to book passage across a lake, let alone a sea. Perhaps it would be best to disregard the words of Herman, the great seer of the West and evening meal of a dragon. But something nagged at him. A little voice, urging him to heed the dead man's last words.

Bruce stayed at the bar, sucking down alternating mugs of good and bad ale until the room started to clear. Olga and Svetlana bustled about the tables, wiping them down and setting out the miniature butter churns in preparation for the breakfast crowd.

He found that if he closed one eye, he had difficulty telling the sisters apart. That alone convinced him it was time to find his bed. He stumbled up the stairs, entered the room with a black ram on the door, and dropped onto the pallet. He yelled as the pain registered. Armor, he'd forgotten to remove his damned armor.

Bruce roused himself to a seated position and fumbled with the straps, laces, and buckles until the metal plating lay beside him along with his sword. He promptly passed out.

An annoyingly bright morning sun beaming through the window onto his face convinced Bruce to get up. He rubbed his bleary eyes and relieved himself out said window in a futile effort to extinguish the light, and then went downstairs. He took a seat on a bench in a dark corner. With his head resting on his hands and his elbows planted on the table to keep him vertical, he tried to block out the buzz of chatter that filled the room.

Water sloshed out of the mug that was slid in front of him, soaking his sleeve. He was about to glare at the careless staff when he saw it was Svetlana. She, more carefully, placed a bowl beside him.

"Hope you slept well," she said.

"I don't recall."

She giggled. It made his stomach flip. Or maybe that was the result of too much ale the night before. One glance at the bowl confirmed that reason was more likely.

"What's for breakfast?"

"Stew."

It was good the night before, but his churning stomach made it quite clear it would not be good now. "How about some bread?"

"Sure." She bustled over to the bar and then returned with a small loaf of brown bread. "Olga churned the butter fresh this morning. I filled the churns. Aren't they cute? Mom is into pottery. She made them."

Bruce imagined Olga spending her morning churning butter and wondered if that was where she got her muscle. "Does your mother help out around the inn too?"

"Oh no, she lives in an artist colony on the outskirts of town. She's allergic to wool."

"That's rather unfortunate, isn't it?"

"Yes, I do miss her so." Svetlana let out a wistful sigh. "When were you planning on leaving? When my father came in last night, I told him of your glorious feat. He was quite impressed. He wanted to speak to you."

"Is that so?" Maybe the wealthy innkeeper wished to donate funds for his trip. Visions of heavy sacks of coins danced through his head, much improving his wellbeing. "I imagine I'll be on my way after lunch. Not good to start out on such an important quest with an empty stomach."

"Certainly. That sounds very wise." She gazed at him with blatant adoration. "I'll send my father over."

Moments later, a man half the height of Bruce, waddled over to the table. He pulled his stocky frame up onto a bench and stroked his thick beard. "Bruce Gawain, is it?"

Bruce nodded, wondering how Svetlana and Olga managed their height despite descending from a dwarf.

"No need to tie your face into a knot over it. The wife's an elf. They get their looks from her. Though, poor Olga ended up on the big-boned side. Not much to be done about it. Should be happy they don't have beards, eh?" He grinned. "Name's Gildersnorf." He held out his stubby hand.

Bruce enveloped the thick, hairy fingers in his grip and pumped the dwarf's hand. "Well met."

"Indeed." Gildersnorf knelt on the bench, giving him the illusion of sitting at the height of a short man. "I hear you're going across the sea."

"It would seem so." The Sea of Sickness. That rather aptly described his stomach about now.

"I have a proposition for you. Being a knight and all, I figure I can trust you. See, I own the Sheep's Inn. A whole chain of them actually, and they're doing quite well. You may have heard of us?"

The question sounded familiar. Bruce racked his blurry mind. "You can count on us?"

Gildersnorf grinned. "Good! I like you already. Well, you see, the market in Holden is pretty much saturated with inns and such these days, and I need to expand."

"I hear there's good money in mining."

The dwarf frowned. "Har, har. No need to be insulting."

Bruce looked around but no one in the sparsely populated room offered insight into his social blunder. "Sorry, I—"

"Look, it's no secret that I'm a dwarf, and yes, I know I'm far outside the stereotype, but hospitality, that's where the big money is."

Bruce didn't recall meeting any hospitable dwarfs in all his travels.

"My family are miners, but when I fell for Timbraelveayia, they cast me out. Ruined a perfectly good race feud, they said. Went against the norm, you know? So, I decided to embrace that sentiment and go into the hospitality market. Shame that Svety had to go and get herself chosen by the sheep god. My wife's wool allergies put a real strain on our family. She's a gifted artist."

Gildersnorf pulled a clay sheep from a pouch around his waist. "Look at this, will ya?" He set it down gently on the table.

Bruce blinked and focused on the fist-sized, clay sheep with an opening cut into its back. "What is the slot for?"

"Coins. I'm trying out a new marketing technique." He held the clay sheep aloft. "Look at all the money ewe've saved by staying with us!" He set the sheep back down. "See, customers can save all their extra coins they would have spent by staying elsewhere right in this handy sheep, which will remind them of us. Pretty good, eh?"

"Very witty." Bruce shoved the last of his bread into his mouth and tried to think of a polite way to excuse himself.

Gildersnorf took in the exodus of the bread and cleared his throat. "Anyway, expanding, yes. See, Holden is full of Inns. But Gambreland is a virtually untouched market."

Bruce mumbled around the bread in his mouth, "Might have to do with the Plains of Pain and Forest of Forgetfulness."

"That's Forest of Fear."

"Right, sorry, I get those confused."

"The Forest of Forgetfulness is on the Misty Isle. And the Plains of Pain? I haven't heard of those." Gildersnorf cocked a bushy eyebrow. "Are you sure you know where you're going?"

"I'll figure it out."

The dwarf nodded. "That's what maps are for, eh? The reason I wanted to talk to you is that I want to expand."

"So you've said." Like three times now, Bruce mumbled to himself.

"Right, well I can't leave Holden right now. Pressing meetings to attend to, you know?"

Bruce didn't have a clue what the rambling dwarf was talking about. "And I'm going to stop you there. I already have a quest. I'm booked for now, but if I'm passing through at a later—"

"I'd like you to take Svetlana. She's got a good eye for location."

"I'd love to take her." His imagination leaped into action as did another part of his anatomy. "Yes, I could definitely work that into my schedule."

Gildersnorf's bushy brows scrunched low and his voice took in an annoyed edge. "That means you'll be taking Olga too. Though I trust your honor as a knight, I can't have my dear Svety defiled. She'll keep you all fed on your journey as long as you keep her safe."

Bruce sighed. "And what do I get out of this arrangement?"

"I'll pay for your sea passage."

"You've got a deal." He shook the dwarf's hand. It might have not been bags of gold, but he needed to get to Gambreland one way or another and free sounded pretty darn good.

"Wait, what about getting back? I mean, you don't expect me to pay for return fare for both of your daughters, do you?"

"Of course not." I'll give Olga enough to see them safely home. And if they have a good report, you come see me when your back in town. I'll reward you for your service."

"Sounds good." Bruce's fingers worried the last two coins left in his pouch. "Not that I don't appreciate the offer of paid passage and a reward upon safe return, but I do need a few supplies for the journey. A small advance would be most helpful."

Gildersnorf grumbled, but dug into the pouch at his thick waist and came out with three silver coins. He dropped them into Bruce's open hand with a look that implied he wasn't about to offer anything more.

"Many thanks," said Bruce. "I'll meet your daughters back here for lunch." He rose from the bench and returned to his room. When he'd donned his armor and strapped on his sword, he took a walk back to the marketplace.

It might not be an official quest, but it was a paying job, and then there was the whole Wall of Nok thing. Was that a side quest, a mission, a journey, or an adventure? Hazy definitions whirled around in his mind as he traversed the mess of several flattened stalls. The rest remained standing and business seemed to be just as bustling as it had been the day before, pre-dragon. A few passersby pointed and waved to him. He waved back with a smile and nod to each one. He might have nodded off during the lesson on what defined an official quest, but he did remember the guidelines of retaining a good social following.

Bruce spent the morning enjoying the fresh air, which helped clear the previous night's overindulgence from his system. He purchased some food to supplement Svetlana's endless mutton supply, a nice new pack in which to carry said food, a shiny new dagger with an engraved bone hilt, and two new shirts. Wearing his armor while at sea wasn't entirely practical and the shirt he normally wore was quite stained. That wouldn't make a good impression on the sisters at all. With nothing more than lint left in his coin purse, he headed back to the inn. Gildersnorf would be covering his passage and the sisters would have some coins of their own. He was sure he could charm a few off of Svetlana if he needed to. Gambreland would undoubtedly hold its own opportunities.

The sisters joined him for a hearty lunch, at which Gildersnorf graced them with a dwarven tale. His deep voice boomed through the room, drawing the attention of all the patrons.

And so set out the travelers three,
To find gold and wisdom by a tree.
By ship they traveled far and fast,
Til the sea grew angry and broke their mast.
Washed up on a golden shore,

Their clothes torn and little more.
The crew all dead,

"Father," said Olga. "Perhaps this isn't the most auspicious time for that particular tale."

Bruce had to agree, even though the crowd muttered their disapproval over having the tale end just as it was getting started.

Gildersnorf stepped down from the tabletop that had served as his stage. "I'm sorry, my friends, we will continue this tale after these three are on their way. A ship waits at the harbor to take my daughters and this brave knight far from home. May their quests be fruitful!" He raised his mug and pounded down its contents. Ale dribbled down the corners of his mouth and into his beard.

Taking that as a cue to leave, Bruce picked up his pack and looked to the sisters. "Well, we best be off."

After a tearful farewell, Olga slung her bag over her broad shoulder and went over to a chest beside the wall. "You'll have to help me with this," she said to Bruce.

"What's in here?" The sealed wooden chest bore a sturdy-looking padlock.

"Svetlana's clothes. She insisted on taking her entire wardrobe. Father agreed because he wanted her to look good for business meetings."

He strained to lift his end. "We can't carry this all the way to the harbor."

Olga batted her eyelashes. "I thought you were a strong knight?"

"Of course I am. But if my arm is tired from carrying this chest, how can I be at my best to protect you and your beautiful sister as your father has charged me to do?"

"I see your point." Her lips twitched. "It's a good thing father insisted on hiring a cart. You *can* drive a cart?"

Bruce glared at her. "Of course, I can drive a cart."

"How was I supposed to know? It's not like you showed up here on some magnificent steed. Or any steed for that matter. What kind of knight travels around the country on foot? One who can't ride, I'd say."

"I happen to be between horses right now, all right? It's no big deal. Happens to people all the time."

"If you say so."

He didn't like the way she always seemed to be on the verge of laughing at him. A knight deserved respect.

"The wagaon's waiting outside," she said.

They hoisted the chest between them and fumbled their way out the door. Svetlana joined them moments later, wiping tears from her flushed cheeks. She sniffled and climbed up onto the seat next to her sister.

Bruce took the reins and gave them a snap. The

horses looked back at him and uttered annoyed protests. He tried again with less snap. They started forward at a lazy pace. One let loose a cloud of gas that made his eyes water. The sisters did not appear to notice. Could horses aim that sort of thing? He gave them another firm thwack of the reins. They finally got moving along.

Halfway to the docks, a large shadow drifted over the cart, and the street, and the houses. People screamed and pointed to the sky. Bruce hunched down in his armor and urged the horses to go faster.

Svetlana shrieked, "Dragon!"

Olga cast him an accusing glare. "That wouldn't be the same Dragon you defeated yesterday, would it?"

Bruce steered the horses through the weaving chaos of bodies. "I never used the word *defeated*."

"So you wounded it then?"

He gritted his teeth. Did getting his coin stuck in the dragon's teeth count as wounding? "Maybe."

Olga's irate voice cut through the screams of the fleeing crowds. "Maybe? You don't even know what you did to the dragon?"

"It left. Isn't that the important thing?"

"No! Now it's back! What are you planning to do about that, oh brave knight?" Olga yanked the reins from his hands. "Go on, save us. I'll even pull over and watch." True to her word, she drew the horses to a halt. Then she gave him a shove, propelling him off the bench seat and onto the street in an ungraceful clanking of armor.

Bruce pulled himself up from the cobbles, felt for his scabbard to make sure it was still at his side, and readied his tirade for the annoying woman.

Her eyebrows raised, she regarded him, and then she thrummed her fingers on the seat in slow succession. "Anytime now."

He let out a sigh. Spinning around, in what he considered a perfectly executed theatrical move, he put his hand on the pommel of his sword and faced the dragon swooping overhead.

"Ho, Dragon," he yelled. "What is it you seek?"

The long neck of the dragon snapped in his direction, throwing its body off balance. It fluttered in the air for a moment and then dove toward him. Bruce's wrist nearly snapped as he tried to draw his sword. It refused to budge. He whipped around to face Olga.

"Foolish woman! You bent my scabbard and now my sword is locked in it! Give me yours!"

Olga shrugged. "Ladies don't carry swords. Borrow one. That's what I always do."

He growled and turned back to the great gusts of air buffeting him as the dragon dropped to the street. Its wings whipped him with dirt, pelting his face and eyes with tiny projectiles. He held up his hands to block his face, fully expecting to feel the dragon's teeth pierce his armor at any given second.

"I have a name, you know. Jaskernect. You could try using that instead of *Dragon*."

Hot breath wafted over Bruce as the dragon settled onto the ground. "Oh, it's you! Good to see you again."

Bruce wished to disappear, for the dragon to take at least one snap at him, something, anything more menacing than going right for pleasantries. He coughed and wiped the grit from his eyes. "You too, Jaskernect. Why do you insist on terrorizing these people?"

"One of them stole my treasure. I'll keep eating them, one by one until the guilty party returns what they stole."

"You just want it returned? No punishment for the thief?"

Jaskernect shrugged its powerful shoulders. "I might eat the thief. But I'd not bother anyone else. I prefer my food less...fishy. Everyone here reeks of them."

"Fair enough." He turned to the scuffling of hundreds of feet behind him. People with slack jaws peered over the cart and out from around corners of homes and shops. "Hear that? You turn over the thief and the stolen treasure, and the dragon will leave your town alone."

Murmurs rolled through the crowd and the people began to disperse.

Bruce grinned at the dragon. "See, there, you'll

have your treasure back in no time. No need to bother these fine folks any longer."

Jaskernect cast a skeptical glance over the retreating people.

"You'll see. It will all work out. Now, why don't you just go wait in the courtyard over there?" He pointed to a large cobbled yard they'd just passed. "I'm sure that will be more comfortable for you. There's a nice fountain there if you get thirsty."

"That sounds quite nice." The dragon thumped its way toward the wide-open space. It then curled up next to the fountain and called out, "You hear that? I'll be waiting right here for my treasure and my thief meal or I'll suffer my way through devouring all of your fishy flesh."

With the danger averted, Bruce strode back to the cart and the two wide-eyed sisters.

Svetlana stammered, "Did the dragon really talk?"

"Are they not supposed to?" Bruce took the reins from Olga's trembling hands and spurred the horses into action.

She shook her head. I've never heard of one plainly talking like that before. I thought they had their own language. The tales always have them speak in riddles."

Bruce shrugged. "Maybe the tales aren't always true. Besides, it will be long gone before we even reach the shores of Gambreland. You won't have to worry about dragons, talking or otherwise, ever again."

Olga seemed to snap out of her daze. "You talked to it before, didn't you? You didn't fight it off, you just talked to it!"

"Lucky for you, I'd say, since you managed to bend my scabbard. You could have gotten us all killed."

Olga lowered her voice a smidgen. "What did you say to it the first time to make it leave?"

Bruce considered his choice of truthful answers and decided he'd admitted enough for one day. "I was merely polite. Must everything be about fighting and swords? Why is talking out a problem so looked down upon? Would you rather cheer over bloodshed than give peace a chance?"

Svetlana clutched her hands on her lap and let out an adoring sigh. She batted her long lashes at him.

"You have odd ideals for a knight," said Olga.

He concentrated on the road. The harbor came in to view, tall masts rocking to and fro, blue waters stretching as far as he could see, and shore birds flying high in the sky. "So, what ship did your father charter for us?"

Svetlana chewed her lip. Then her eyes lit up. "The Driftwood."

"You've got to be kidding," said Bruce.

"What? Do you know that ship?" asked Svetlana.

"No, and I'm not sure I want to." Bruce began to reconsider the offer of free passage as he pulled the cart to a halt. He hopped down to help the sisters out. Olga declined his assistance, jumping down beside him.

Bruce held up his hand to Svetlana. She slipped into his arms with a giggle and dropped to her feet.

"Driftwood floats. The name makes perfect sense to me." Svetlana shrugged and pointed to the chest. "Don't forget my things."

"It also implies that our ship will be smashed into a thousand tiny bits to be washed up on the shore," Bruce said.

Svetlana giggled. "But think of all the firewood we'd be providing for the poor who live along the shoreline. And really, there's nothing more romantic than a bonfire on the beach."

Olga cocked her head. "Hard to enjoy that romantic moment when you're dead at the bottom of the sea, isn't it?"

Svetlana turned to Bruce.

"I have to agree with Olga on this one," he said.

"Fine, neither of you would know a romantic thought if it hit you on the head." She spun around. "Bring my trunk."

Bruce and Olga hefted the chest between them and walked down the long dock. The cries of birds greeted them along with the lapping of waves and shouts of men loading the ship. Crates and sacks traveled up the gangplank on the backs of hunched men, reminding Bruce of a trail of ants. They grunted beneath their loads while those on deck called out in encouragement.

A man who stood a head taller than Bruce stepped into their path. "You must be our passengers."

Svetlana dodged around their crate to greet the captain. She handed him a letter from her father.

The captain gave her an appreciative once over then noticed Bruce. His gaze returned to Svetlana and a charming smile broke out on his face. Olga stepped between, arms crossed over her chest. The captain quickly returned his attention to the letter, cracking the seal and scanning the message.

"Go on then," he said, waving them to the end of the line waiting to board the gangplank. As he walked back to his men, the large plume on his tri-cornered hat blew in the slight breeze. Bruce envied his easy walk, unencumbered by armor. Though, he didn't welcome the thought of carrying all his armor as well as the crate. It was just plain easier to wear it. He found himself sweating with the extra exertion of handling the heavy load. He sneaked a glance at Olga. Not a drop of sweat on her. Smiling even. Bruce grumbled under his breath.

The walk up the plank was tenuous. By the time they made it onboard, his arms were shaking. He sighed with relief when Olga suggested they set their burden down.

The captain shook his head. "You'll have to stow that below deck. Find a spot in the storeroom. I'll not be responsible for damage to your belongings if you leave that up here. One of my men will show you to your cabin—my own, actually. Only the best for the daughters of Gildersnorf." He flashed them a wide grin of half-rotten teeth.

Svetlana grimaced.

As their guide led them to the pulley, Bruce turned around to whisper to her. "You can't expect seamen to have good oral health. I'm sure it is quite low on their list of priorities, what with all the hoisting of sails, coiling of ropes, and keeping their ship from getting smashed to bits to provide romantic bonfires for the poor."

Tears came to her eyes. "I just realized what daddy meant about missing my smile."

Bruce and Olga set the crate down next to the hole leading to the storeroom below where two men were working with a winch and pulley to lower supplies.

Svetlana stepped between them. "Don't you get it? The Sea of Sickness? Don't you know the effects of bile on teeth?" Tears rolled down her cheeks. "Not only do I have to leave home and Daddy, but I'm also going to lose my fetching smile."

Bruce patted her shoulder. "I assure you, you have plenty of other assets to make up for it."

Olga stomped on his foot. A metallic twang filled

the air as her calfskin boot met his plate boot. Tears came to her eyes too.

It was the first time in weeks Bruce was happy to be wearing armor. He watched Olga try to be inconspicuous as she rubbed her foot. He smiled to himself. "Who knows if we'll even be sick? I mean, it looks like any other water to me. What could happen?"

❦ 2 ❦

Olga Has No Respect For Knights

Olga stepped off the dock and dropped to her knees on the lush green grass. For the first time in twenty-three days, she didn't have the urge to vomit, though tears came to her eyes nevertheless.

The call of *Baaaaaaaaa* filled the air. Svetlana herded the thirteen sheep down the dock and into the grass where they milled about and chewed heartily. With her head finally clearing of the wretched haze that had enveloped it from the moment they lost sight of the shores of Holden, Olga paused to do the math. Twenty-three days, four sheep slaughtered for meals that were summarily heaved over the deck rails left six sheep unaccounted for.

"Svety, come here a moment." She glanced at the dock where Bruce and one of the crewmen fought with the crate.

Svetlana warned her sheep to stay close and came to her sister's side. "What is it?"

Olga looked her sister over. Thinner, which made her curves even more apparent, a bit gaunt in the face and smiling. No, glowing. "Svetlana! What have you done?"

Her sister blushed. "The captain was angry about another sheep showing up every morning. It seems father left that detail out of his letter. We couldn't eat them all, obviously." She shrugged. "Tossing them overboard was just plain cruel. The captain feared retribution from animal rights activists at their trade ports if word got out, and while there was a bit of food on board for the sheep, the ship wasn't provisioned to support all the additional animals. We were running out of room. The constant bleating was driving everyone crazy. You said so yourself, more than once."

Svetlana turned away from her sister to look at the sheep grazing. "To resolve the situation, Bruce and I decided the best option was to end production of the sheep."

Olga felt her mouth drop open. "You slept with Bruce?"

Svetlana turned back to her sister and grinned. "Oh yes. Several times. We wanted to make sure there would be no more sheep. It wouldn't do to have the captain even angrier with us."

"The *captain*?" Olga's voice rose to a point where her throat hurt. "You were worried about a captain we'll likely never see again? What about our father? Our mother? Our inns? Svetlana, what have you done?"

Bruce approached with tiptoeing steps, nodding to his helper to set the crate down. "Now, Olga, I know you're probably angry." He put his pack on his shoulder and held out his empty hands.

"Probably? You've ruined our family. Father trusted you!"

"And I've seen you safe to Gambreland, just like I promised. Had I not taken action with Svetlana, the captain may have put us off at the nearest port. He threatened to. You didn't hear that part of the conversation though, did you? Too busy vomiting over the side of the ship, I bet."

Her hands rose to her hips. "So were you! We all were!"

Bruce said, "Well, I happened to be vomiting next to the captain. I heard his every word."

"And now, what are we going to eat? We're stuck here, for who knows how long it is going to take Svetlana to seek out prospective business sites."

He gave her an odd look. "What do you mean *we*? I'm traveling to the Wall of Nok. I got you here. That was the deal. I protected your sister on the journey. And I did a better job of it than you did, I'll say."

Olga wiped the smug look off his face with a fist

to his jaw. She watched with great satisfaction as he fell on his behind, his armor crunching and rattling. "You ruined her! You call that doing a better job?" She gave him a kick for good measure and then belatedly remembered his armor. Stupid knight. She limped aside. "You stay away from her."

He clambered to his feet. "Why? What difference does it make now?"

He was grinning again. She hated him. She balled her fist and readied another punch.

"Olga," Svetlana laid a hand on her shoulder, "don't hurt Brucey. He's so sweet."

Her voice rose to a shrill pitch, "Brucey? Good God, Svety, couldn't you at least have the creativity to come up with something less trite? Honey? Sugar? Even Cuddle Bunny, for goodness' sake?"

Svetlana regarded her with a blank stare. "You'd like him too if you got to know him. He taught me so many things."

"Is that so? Like what?"

"One night Brucey taught me how to climb his mast." She ticked off a finger. "Then there was, hoisting his mainsail, and swabbing his deck." She ticked off two more. "Then we discussed pirates and he demonstrated pillaging, and—"

Olga slammed her hands over her ears. "I don't want to hear it!" She stalked away before she hurt either of them permanently.

The tall green grass was a welcome sight after

the weeks at sea. Waves still reverberated in her ears, and the solid ground still felt as if it were rocking to and fro but at least the cursed nausea had come to an end. The lack of keeping anything down had defined her muscles but that wasn't really the look she was going for. It was bad enough to have Daddy's bone structure. Then there was keeping herself in shape to defend Svetlana's honor. Now she didn't even have that. She was just a big girl that now *really* looked like a man.

Her lip quivered. She bit down on it. There would be none of that. Enough tears had been shed over her lack of husbandly prospects and nun-like future. She froze. Wait, if she no longer had to guard her sister, that meant she was free!

Olga raised her face to the weak sunlight peeking through the murky grey clouds. Maybe Svety's loss of virginity wasn't such a bad thing after all. She could stop working out, see what kind of body she'd end up with. Maybe a man would come along that wouldn't mind her giant dwarfish bones. Still, she didn't plan on forgiving either of them any time soon.

She whipped around to address Svetlana, "And just how do you plan on feeding us while we're here?"

Bruce stepped forward. "Your dear sister and I were discussing that very matter just last night in bed."

Olga held up her hand. "I don't want to hear about it."

"Right, sorry. Anyway, we were discussing the food issue, and there doesn't seem any reason why she can't keep this herd of sheep and breed them. They are blessed sheep, right? Gifts from the Sheep God? So why not market them as such. Keep a core stock and maybe sell off a few here and there for breeding purposes. Spread the godly bloodlines and such. You could get a fortune for each one that way, much more than you get by selling them for food. And once they're a breeding bunch, you could harvest all the holy wool and start an exclusive clothing line. That way the Sheep's Inn name still applies." He held up his hands as if illustrating a sign. "Holy woolen socks and cloaks. Crowds would come from miles around to stock up on their winter wear. Think about it."

"Are you sure you didn't steal all that from Svetlana?"

Her sister shook her head. "Not only is he a dashing knight, but he also has a head for business. Won't Daddy be so happy?"

Olga snorted. "Not one bit, no."

But his ideas, if they were truly his, sounded logical enough. They might have merit. Svetlana seemed to think they did, and she was the one with the mind for business, if not much else. Svety seemed gifted with that one thing. Bruce, she didn't know that well. From the look of him, a successful businessman, he was not.

Like Bruce, swords and poking things with them were Olga's gifts. Maybe she could enjoy her time away from home, decide what she wanted to do with her life. Svetlana didn't need her anymore. Her father didn't need her to guard her sister. Mother, Olga sighed, she'd never had much use for her big daughter anyway—her hands more suited for a weapon or farm work than fine artistry.

She kicked at a clump of grass and waded in further. "So, Svety, which way to the first town?"

Her sister peered up at the sun and then looked around. "East, I think. Should be a day inland."

Bruce caught up to them, though he stayed a pace or two behind. "That far inland? Why wouldn't they have a town here by the port?"

"Looks like there was one once." Olga pointed to the burnt remains of buildings. Sand crept around the blackened timbers.

"I wonder what happened here." Svetlana pursed her lips. "This was on the map Daddy showed me. He claimed it was up to date."

"Apparently not," Bruce wandered past them and into the grass.

Olga followed. The rustling of grass accompanied by the occasional bleating of sheep kept them company. Ten minutes later she stopped and smacked her forehead. "We forgot something."

Svetlana looked around, "What?"

Bruce grumbled and hung his head. "The crate."

"I thought you were just stretching your legs," said Svetlana. "I didn't realize we were actually starting off or I would have mentioned it sooner."

Olga again resisted the urge to slap her sister. "Let's go." She set off at a brisk pace with Bruce close behind. Her sister and her sheep lagged in the distance. "We're not carrying that damned thing for an entire day."

"I thought you said it wasn't heavy?" said Bruce.

"I thought I told you to shut up."

They glared at one another until Olga broke away. She said, "If you can wear your armor, she can wear whatever she needs."

"Good point." Bruce nodded.

The crate sat at the edge of the grass where they had left it. She waved at Bruce. "Go ahead, open it."

"Me? Why do I want an eyeful of your sister's underthings?"

"Oh please. You've no doubt seen it all before. Get to it."

"And just what do you expect me to open it with? It's nailed shut."

Olga shrugged. "Use your sword."

"Are you kidding? That would ruin my sword."

"It's not much use if you can't even draw it, is it? If we get into a situation, I'm sure you can talk your way out of it. You seem to be good at that." She pointed to the crate. "Just open the thing already."

He tugged and wrestled with the sword until he

got it out of the scabbard. "Fine, but you're going to regret this."

"It's not the first thing I'll regret about this trip." She stood back and watched Bruce pry up the edges.

When he'd finished, he held up the dented and bent sword and beheld it with a look of utter dismay. "I've had this sword for a long time. Now it's worthless."

She almost felt bad for him. Almost. "Maybe we'll come across a blacksmith that can fix it up for you. I'll even pay for the repairs."

"Really?" A gleam of hope returned to his eyes.

Olga nodded and then peered inside. A single change of her clothing sat neatly folded in one corner. Two dresses and a cloak lay spread out over the rest. She heard Svetlana come up behind her. "How many dresses did you need to bring? And what are they made of, stone?"

"No, silly, daddy wanted me to bring a few things to hand out in prospective towns."

A sinking feeling in her stomach told Olga what she would likely find under the clothing. She lifted a corner of the cloak. Sure enough, layers upon layers of neatly packed clay sheep.

Bruce swore.

Olga turned to glare at her sister but found that Svetlana had developed a sudden interest in the wellbeing of her sheep. She glanced up at her sister after a long silence. "It was Daddy's idea."

"Then Daddy can carry them across all of Gambreland. I sure don't plan on it."

"But Mom made them special." She pulled one out of the crate. "See, they have tiny portraits of Daddy on them. If you look closely, you can see he's got a sheep under one arm and he's holding a banner emblazoned with Gambreland's seal in the other. She hand-painted each one. They're a limited special run. Collector's items."

Olga had never liked sheep all that much, and today, she truly began to loathe them. "How about we get to this town you're aiming for, and you send someone back with a cart and have *them* pick this crate up?"

"That might cost an awful lot. How much did daddy give you?" asked Svetlana.

"Enough. But just to be safe, how about you offer to pay those helpful folks with special limited edition clay sheep."

Svetlana tapped her chin for a moment. "Say, that's not a bad idea."

"Good. Then how about we take our clothes and get out of here. It will be dusk within an hour or two, and I'd like to get away from the shore to somewhere a bit more sheltered."

The grassland gave way to scraggly trees around the time the sun turned to orange on the horizon. Olga glanced about. "Good enough. Gather up some wood so we can have a fire. Oh, and what all do you have in that pack of yours, Bruce?"

"Food. Since we didn't eat much on the ship, I have plenty left. I could share...I guess."

Olga raised an eyebrow and shook her head. "You bet you guess. I hope it's the good kind of food."

Bruce gave her a dry smile. "Yeah, it's the kind you eat."

"My favorite. Get a fire started and let's dig in."

The knight sighed and went about gathering up branches. When he had a sizeable stack nearby, he sat down and started cracking smaller sticks into little pieces. "So who has the flint?"

Svetlana looked to Olga.

Olga shook her head. "You had that entire crate, and you didn't think to pack flint in it? You've got to be kidding." She turned to Bruce. "And you, a knight with that bulging pack of yours, not a speck of flint?"

"I've got some somewhere, I was just hoping one of you could offer some help here." He muttered and reached for his pack. "Both of you just sitting around while the man in heavy armor gathers the wood, and stacks the wood, and sets up the fire, and starts the fire, and hands out the food." He glanced up at Olga as if to make sure she was getting all of his rant. "When I purchased my supplies, I'd only planned to feed one, not three."

"We've got thirteen sheep. Pick one and call it yours for all I care."

Bruce gazed into the settling dusk. "I can't do

that. Svety needs her sheep to get a good start on her blessed flock."

At least the man had some thought about seeing that her sister was taken care of. "So when are the two of you planning to be wed?"

Bruce made a choking noise. "I'm sorry, what was that you said?"

"Married. When are you planning to marry my sister? You break it, you buy it. You know?"

"Uhhh. Let me think on that. I need to take a short walk anyway." Bruce got up and wandered into the grass.

Olga spotted her sister nearby. "Svety, how are the sheep?"

"Just fine." She sat by Olga, spreading her skirt out in perfect ladylike fashion.

Olga regarded her leggings and sleeveless jerkin. Someday, she wanted to fit into a nice dress. Her work uniform was the only feminine wear she owned. Otherwise, she wore what she wore today—clothes more suited to the farm chores.

Svetlana gazed up at the first stars. "What's for dinner?"

"I don't know. Check in Bruce's pack."

"Where is it?"

"Right there." Olga pointed across the unlit heap of sticks. The pack was gone. And so was Bruce. She listened hard. Nothing. "He's run off!"

Svetlana let out a shrill, "Brucey!"

Nothing.

"See, Svety, this is why you don't sleep with men. They leave after they get what they want."

Svetlana sobbed. "But why would my Brucey leave? He seemed so happy."

"Oh, I'm sure he did. They always do. They tell you they are happy and that they love you, but the moment you mention commitment, they run."

Her sister sniffed. "But I never mentioned commitment. You did."

Olga checked the stars rather than meet the accusing glare she felt emanating from her sister. "Well, he's gone."

Svetlana got to her feet. "Then let's go find him."

"Your sheep aren't going to like traveling at night. We'll have to wait until morning."

"So we're going to just sit here while my Brucey is getting away?"

Olga cringed. "Please don't say that name again. That no-good knight's name is Bruce. And yes, we're going to spend the night here. His tracks will be easy enough to find in the grass."

"Fine." Svetlana crossed her arms over her ample chest and pouted.

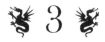

Svetlana Hearts Bruce

"Brucey!" Svetlana yelled into the crisp morning air. She knew, despite what Olga said, that Brucey wouldn't just leave. Not after all they'd shared.

Olga scowled. "I told you to stop calling him that! Besides, his tracks lead far into the grass ahead of us. If the man is running from us, and he clearly spent a good deal of last night doing so, what makes you think he's going to suddenly have a change of heart and answer you?"

"He said he loved me."

"They all say that, stupid."

"Don't call me stupid!" As if Olga had any idea about the ways of the family business. The only thing she was good for was lugging supplies and milking cows. With Brucey's great idea, the family business would be fine, or even better than fine. If only Olga could see past the lost virginity factor.

That didn't seem like much of a loss to Svetlana. Maybe Olga was just jealous. Being the older sister and still a virgin might be hard for her to bear. Poor thing. It wasn't as if she had suitors lining up back home. There'd never been even the start of a line. If she wasn't mad about being called stupid, she might have hugged her sister.

"Why are you looking at me like that?" snarled Olga.

"No reason." Svetlana left her sister to her bad mood and gazed at the clear path in the grass. Wherever Brucey was headed, he was on a mission. Perhaps Olga's talk of commitment sent him off to the town to send a cart back for the two of them, or maybe he went to find whatever passed for the local holy man. Yes, that must be it. Svetlana patted the head of the nearest sheep and trounced along Brucey's path.

Olga glanced over her shoulder, her face still set in a deep frown. "What are you smiling about?"

"Just enjoying the walk." Her sister was not a fan of Brucey. The two of them would have to come up with some ideas to sway Olga. She glanced down at her sheep. "Come on, we have a long journey ahead."

A braying voice spoke in her head. *"OoOoour feet are tired."*

"Mine too." She stroked the ram's wooly coat.

Olga let out an exasperated sigh. "You're talking

to them now?"

Svetlana nodded, motioning Olga to be quiet.

"We are glad you ended this plight upoOoon us. OoOoour numbers were dwindling in the heavens. NoOoot to mention knowing that your father murdered so many of OoOoour kind."

Tears came to Svetlana's eyes. The price for giving up the gift of the Sheep God was that now she could hear them. She knew their pain, their suffering, and their anger at being sent from heaven, not to be plentiful upon the earth as they had been promised, but to be eaten by man. She wondered if they screamed when they were killed. And would she hear it? She wiped the tear away before Olga saw it and misunderstood her emotional moment.

"We are joOooyful for the one called Bruce. He is a wise man. He will be blessed by our GoOood."

"Not by sending more sheep, I hope?"

"NoOoooo, we will come up with an approOoopriate reward."

"Sounds good. Now, let's go find my Brucey." Svetlana picked up the pace. The sheep overtook Olga, plowing a wide path along Bruce's far narrower one.

Olga let out a frustrated growl. "Get them back here. They are going to obliterate the trail."

"Sorry." Svetlana took off after her eager sheep. Touched with a twitch of jealousy, she wondered if the sheep liked Brucey better than her. Could they speak to him too? Probably not, she decided. Else they would have said something to her about that. Wouldn't they?

Once she caught up to the sheep, she did her best to slow them down. They didn't seem to listen to her like they had before. It took her a while to gather them all back into an orderly flock so she could preserve the trail for Olga.

The sun was high overhead when she got the idea to pull out her map. She called for Olga to wait.

"He's going to the town where we're going."

"Of course he is." Olga gave her that look she hated that said she was being dense. "There isn't anywhere else to go other than off into the wilderness around here."

"Then why do we need this trail?"

Olga peered over the grass, scanning their surroundings. "Have you noticed the other trails?"

Svetlana took her attention from the sheep to see what Olga was talking about. A much narrower trail wove alongside this one. It wasn't a straight line at all, and not as clear. There might have also been one on her right. Grass seemed trampled in places there as well.

"What made them do you think?" she asked.

"I don't know, but maybe Bruce was following them."

A burst of happiness shot through Svetlana. "So, you think he didn't run off after all. He's a knight.

He's probably off protecting someone right this instant."

"Maybe." Olga took a long drink from the intricately stamped and painted waterskin their mother had made for them and then handed it to Svetlana. "But I rather doubt it."

Angry at her sister's doubt, she declined the drink and started off again on the trail. She held her head high as she walked. "We'll catch up to him soon enough, and then you'll see just what a great man he really is."

❧ 4 ❧

Bleating Ewegene

The town came into view when the sun was well into its downward arc in the sky.

Ewegene glanced over at Ramses. "Where are we going? We're leaving the chosen one behind."

He nodded and plodded onward, letting out an occasional bleat for that sake of appearance. "We cannot afford to send more of our number to this cursed plane. Our god ignores our plight. He's too smitten with the girl. We will follow a new chosen one. Did you hear his plans? He doesn't want to eat us."

Ewegene bleated. "Our god will be angry."

"He will be without sheep if we don't. Without us, he will cease to be. It's for his own good." Ramses nuzzled her cheek. "The knight will keep us safe."

"What will we tell our god when he asks about

her?" asked Ewegene. She took one last backward look at the grasslands where they'd left the girl.

"We will tell him the truth. If I have to report one more day about how pretty she is, or how she moves, smells, or what she's wearing, I'll—" He let out a loud and long bleat.

Ewegene couldn't disagree with that. "He'll thank us someday."

"Until then, let's enjoy our freedom. As long as we grow wool, this chosen one will be pleased. We can replenish our numbers again." Ramses gave her a playful wink.

The thought of lambs put a spring in her step. It had been far too long since they'd had young among them.

"How will we honor the new chosen one?" she asked.

Noting a chill in the air, Ramses bared his grass-stained teeth. "I have just the thing."

"I shall leave it to you and our god then." Ewegene curtsied.

❧ 5 ❧

Mydeara Seeks A Sheep

Mydeara peered out the open window. The smell of sweat and urine filled the air. The other townsfolk kept a wary eye on the surrounding grasslands as they went about their business, preparing evening meals and closing down shops for the day. Her father would be sending her younger brother in to wash his hands any minute.

The knight that had wandered into town this morning now sat near the fountain. Sweat rolled down his finely-chiseled nose to drip on his full lips. A dusting of dark hair lined his broad jaw. The light breeze teased his hair. She sighed wistfully and hoped that one day she'd have a husband even half as handsome.

He'd been hungry, and she'd had the pleasure of cooking lunch for him. Him and his smile. Mydeara blushed.

The fountain didn't work. It hadn't in years. With the grasslands filled with wild beasts, travelers from the docks had stopped coming. Caravans no longer stopped. Business had all but come to a standstill.

But the knight had made it through. And a herd of sheep had shown up at the edge of the village an hour ago. If a man traveling alone had made it through the grasslands, as well as the sheep, maybe the beasts had gone away.

She looked to the empty pan near the clay oven. Dinner wouldn't prepare itself. With a sigh, Mydeara pulled herself away from the view and went back to chopping carrots.

A ruckus outside caught her attention. Shouts and running feet. Mydeara grabbed her pan by the handle and held it behind her back, ready to take a swing at anyone who tried to cause trouble for her.

A cry rose higher than the rest. "There are more of them!"

More beasts. The creatures of nightmares. A chill settled over Mydeara. Her fingers wrapped tighter around the pan handle. Would they invade the town? She again glanced around the room, this time hoping to catch some sight or sound of her father in the doorway that led to their shop. Nothing. Mydeara crept to the doorway and looked outside.

People! Not beasts, but more people. They seemed excited to see the sheep. The animals must have belonged to them and perhaps escaped.

Fresh meat. Her stomach rumbled. The beasts had eaten the herd animals months ago. The only cows existed in barns, released into the center of town in the afternoons. They were precious for their milk, not to be eaten. A few goats lived with the old crone down the way. They only lived thanks to the old woman keeping them in her home like children, taking them for walks under her watchful eye. The other eye wasn't so watchful, all cloudy and almost white as it was, but the goats remained among the living nevertheless. Mydeara's hutch of rabbits had been among the first casualties. Their horse followed soon after, along with the family's single cow. Without meat, they'd come to rely on the garden plots every family had expanded this summer. If she had to eat another meal of turnips and carrots, she would scream.

Baaaa.

Saliva pooled in Mydeara's mouth. "Here sheepy sheepy", she said under her breath. She swore one of the sheep glared at her.

A pretty young woman gazed at the gathered crowd. "Have any of you seen a knight?"

The baker stepped forward and pointed to the fountain. "Sure, he's right over there."

Only the knight wasn't there. Mydeara searched the crowd. In fact, the knight was nowhere to be seen.

The young woman peered at the fountain and

raised her brows. "Really? Is he invisible?"

The baker turned around. "He was right there, I swear."

A large man, no, it was a woman. Maybe. Mydeara squinted to make out the details of the brute. Breasts. A woman then. Rather homely, though with an envious head of long blonde hair. Mydeara ran a hand through her dark shorn locks and wondered what it would be like to have long hair. The elders frowned upon such a thing, unclean, they called it. As if anything in this town were clean anymore.

The brute didn't appear to have a weapon. Neither did the pretty one. Yet, they'd made it through the grasslands. They must be free of the beasts at last!

Breezing past the pretty one, the big woman looked around and said, "So Bruce is about then. Good enough. I'm starving. Where might we buy a meal?"

The village scribe took a few tentative steps in her direction, looking much like a terrified mouse. "Might I inquire as to what you wish with the knight? Is he trouble?"

Stepping up, the younger woman bumped the large one aside with the sway of her hip as she passed. "Brucey wouldn't cause any problems. He's a hero and a great knight. It's just that we were separated in the grasslands last night."

The big blacksmith nodded. "By the beasts no doubt."

"I'm Svetlana." She proffered her hand to the blacksmith.

He looked at it and then at her. "I'm Bjorn. Did you see the beasts?"

She squinched up her nose. "Umm, no?"

The sheep meandered away from the fountain.

"Big creatures, large as a horse? Black as night and covered with shaggy, long hair? Teeth the size of your hand and sharp as a knife?"

She shook her head. "Nope."

A cheer went up through the gathered people. "We're free!"

The larger woman spoke up, "Is that why the settlement down by the docks is deserted?"

Bjorn gazed out into the waving grass. "Yes. They ate most of our folk that lived there. Only a few made it back here alive."

"Where did these creatures come from?"

"A ship, we think. A deserted boat was found at the docks last spring. No crew to speak of. No bodies. No cargo. Infested with these things, most likely. Someone must have set their plight afloat, and now we are stuck with this plague."

The big woman smiled. "Does anyone have a sword?"

"Olga, no. We have business to attend to. We're not here to run off on quests. Leave that to Brucey."

"Your beloved *Bruce*," she enunciated his name with care, "is nowhere to be found. You go about your business and leave the questing to me. You don't need me anymore. Bruce saw to that."

The blacksmith smiled at Olga. "I might have a sword that would suit you. Not that you'll need it if the beasts are gone, but we can see if it is a good match for you anyway."

Olga smiled back. "I have a feeling your sword might be. First, I would like to buy something to eat. We've had a long walk from the docks."

The woman had said *buy*. Mydeara's father would beat her if she didn't make an effort to earn a coin. She walked into the crowd, waving her frying pan, but before she could offer up another meal, the baker's wife took Svetlana by the arm and led the two women toward her home.

Well, if she couldn't get paid, she'd get a sheep. Mydeara smiled to herself. While everyone else discussed the absence of the beasts, she slunk away to see where the sheep had gotten off to.

The dirt streets yielded up a clear enough trail of hoof prints that even her brother could have followed. She glanced about, but no one else seemed as interested in the flock as they did with the idea that their plague might be over.

The street dwindled into a somewhat overgrown path in the tall grass as she followed the trail out of the village.

On occasion, she caught a footprint that matched the boots the knight had been wearing. Was he leading the sheep away from the women? She couldn't imagine he would do such a thing. Then again, she barely knew him. Maybe he would.

A distant *baa* drifted to her on the gentle breeze. She walked a little faster.

A man's voice cursed. "Go away."

If there was something out there causing the knight to tell it to go away, she certainly didn't want to face it alone. He would protect her, wouldn't he? That's what knights did, after all.

Mydeara ran through the rolling hills of grass, her breath growing ragged before she spotted the herd of sheep and the knight.

He took a few steps forward. The sheep took a few steps forward. He turned around and glared at them. "I said, go away."

The sheep stood their ground, matching him step for step along the path.

The closer Mydeara got, she realized something about the knight had changed since she saw him last. His thick head of black hair now hung in luscious, curled locks down past his shoulders. Black hair sprouted between the seams of his armor all along his arms, his legs, and even his chest, spilling over at his neck. Thick masses of black curls, everywhere.

"I don't care if it will be a cold night. Your *gift* isn't necessary. I'm glad you're free too, but, really, just go away." His voice teetered on hysteria.

As Mydeara watched, a beard sprouted on his

recently clean-shaven cheeks. When he'd come to town, his face had been scruffy but he'd taken up the offer of a bath and a shave. Now a thick black beard tumbled down his neck to meet the chair at his chest plate. She blinked and rubbed her eyes, but when her vision cleared, the beard remained.

The knight grabbed ahold of the beard and tugged. "What have you done? Leave me alone!" He shook his head, sending a spray of curls flying into the air as if to give Mydeara extra time to appreciate their every gentle movement. "I am not your new chosen one. I'm certainly no virgin. I skipped the day when some of the other knights took that stupid celibacy oath." He backed away and then sprinted down the path, his armor clinking with every heavy footfall.

The herd followed. So did Mydeara. When they again caught up to him, he stood rooted in place with his scabbard in hand.

Mydeara crept through the sheep to his side, her heart pounding. "Sir knight, what's out there?"

"Shhh," he said without turning around, his focus intent on the next hill.

Something moved, and it wasn't just grass. Mydeara grabbed ahold of his armor-covered arm and whispered, "Is it the beasts?"

He tore his gaze from the distance to see her hand and jumped, giving out a little shriek. "Who the—"

"Mydeara, remember? I made you lunch?"

Recognition lit in his eyes. "Oh. What are you doing out here?" He peered over her shoulder. "Are there others with you? Say, three to ten men with swords?"

Whatever was on the hill moved again. The tall grass quivered and then parted.

She shook her head and squeaked, "just me."

"Right." He turned his attention back to the hill and the looming dark shapes that stood upon it. "You don't, by any chance, have a sword or two with you, do you?"

"I can't use a sword with one hand, let alone two." She stepped behind Bruce. His long curls rustled in the breeze. The sheep clustered about her feet.

"I meant for me."

"But you have a sword."

"A useless one." He glared at the sheep. "Yeah, a magical sword would have been much more useful. Brilliant thought. At least I'll be warm as I'm laying here dying."

One of the sheep let out a pathetic bleat. The sound tugged at Mydeara's heart. She reached down to pat the poor creature on the head. "Don't worry," she said, "Bruce is a brave knight. He'll save us all."

The sheep clustered even tighter.

Three giant hairy beasts charged them.

Mydeara screamed. So did Bruce.

Great quaking creatures of black fur bore down

on them with grunts and maniacal shrieking laughter.

Bruce held his scabbard as if it were his sword. Mydeara leaned in closer, her cheeks brushing against the soft hairs flowing from the seams where his arms met the chest plate. Her fingers gripped her pan handle with a force to make her knuckles ache. The sheep backed up a few steps as if to give Bruce room to defend them. She swore she saw the ram at the forefront cringing.

The laughter grew louder. The black fur dropped from the beasts, flowing backward like a cast-off cloak in a heavy wind.

For a split second, she was relieved to discover the beasts weren't demons or some other magical terror as the few who had escaped the beasts had claimed. However, the truth was still dangerous.

Goblins, two apiece, rode atop giant, horned wildebeests. The beasts' beady eyes gleamed. A bubbly froth dripped from their lips as they lowered their head as if ready to charge. The goblins leered at them, their green skin near blending with the grasses but for their gleaming white teeth. And they laughed. And pointed.

❦ 6 ❦

Gols Goes Solo

"See them, you did?" Gols jabbed Hob in the back. "Good we got 'em."

"Did we that." Hob finally stopped laughing. "Scream, he did."

Bup, their captain, raised his hand and pointed to their meal. "We eat!"

Their laughter subsided as hunger took hold. Springing from their mounts, the goblins circled their dinner and pointed their spears inward, trapping their prey.

Gols kicked at the wooly beasts at his feet. Juicy man. Saliva dripped down his chin. Girl child looked tender. He jabbed at her with his spear.

A flat iron round smacked Gols upside the head. His vision blurred. He closed one eye and jabbed again. The man thwacked him in the neck with his hard stick. Gols shrieked and dropped his spear to grasp his throbbing neck. No blood. He reached down to gather up his spear.

The iron met his head again. Stars danced at the edges of his vision. Beside him, Hob called out taunts at their meal. "We eat you. So Tasty!"

Hob and the four others poked the man and girl with their spears. The man glared at their spears and growled angry words Gols didn't understand. Gols hurt. *That* he understood. He stepped back and let the others work. Their mounts rested after their sprint, waiting in the grass.

One of the furry things stepped on his foot. Gols yelped. He kicked at the creature, only to find four more of the white beasts closing in on him. He tried to kick another but found one of them right in front of his legs. The others pressed in, knocking Gols to the ground and swarming on him. Their sharp little hooves dug into his flesh over and over.

Hob went flying through the air, landing near the mounts. He moaned and then fell silent. Gols heard Bup urging the others onward. "Her weapon beware!"

The man's stick landed in the grass beside Gols, hitting one of his furry attackers on the backside. The thing bleated and seemed to glare at the man. That's when Gols noticed that the stick had become a sword. Three of his friends lay dead in the grass.

"Kill him! Our secret he knows." Bup attacked

with new vigor. But he was alone. The sword cut him down.

Evil sword, Gols cursed the man's steel. If only Bup had waited for the rest of the group to return from the shore. But they'd spotted a crate there. The others were convinced there must be food inside. Check it they must, Bup had said. The rest of them had returned to watch for stragglers from the village. Meals had grown thin over the past weeks. The menfolk had grown wise to the goblin threat. They would all go hungry now.

The little hooves disappeared, giving Gols a clear view of the man and his blood-covered sword. He muttered something in man tongue and thrust the steel into Gol's chest. Pain blossomed and deepened as the man twisted the sword and drew it out.

"Baa," said the creature in his face, and then Gols saw no more.

❦ 7 ❦

Harold Of Farnuvia

"A hero!" Harold proclaimed as he ran down the grass-lined path. "I am witness to your great victory. All hail the conqueror of the beasts!"

The very hairy knight and his squire turned from surveying their victory. The squire, Harold realized, upon a longer look, was not a squire at all, but a girl in a skirt holding a long-handled pan at her side.

She returned his gaze levelly. "And just who are you?"

"Why, I am Harold, the renowned bard of Farnuvia. Surely you've heard of me?"

The girl looked him up and down with a scowl. "No."

The knight wiped his sword on the loincloth of one of the slain goblins. "'arold, you say? Nope, haven't heard of you."

"It's Harold." Could the knight not understand him? "From your accent, I gather you're from Holden?"

The knight plucked his scabbard from the grass and slid his sword into it. "Yes, 'arold, I'm Bruce Gawain from 'olden. This is Mydeara." He raised an eyebrow. "And you're one to talk about having an accent."

"I beg your pardon? I do not have an accent."

The girl giggled. "You 'ave one all right. Must be fresh from Farnuvia?"

Harold glared. No doubt about it, they were mocking him. "I was on my way to the next village to gather accounts of survivors of the beast attacks for my next ballad, but since you've conquered the terrifying creatures, your heroic deeds seem far more worthy. My timing is impeccable, as usual," he said proudly. "I'd like to travel with you for a few days, just to see what you're about, while I get the ballad together. If that's all right with you, of course."

Mydeara looked to the knight, tapping the pan against her hip. "Hear that, Bruce? You're a 'ero."

Bruce nodded. "About time someone acknowledges that fact."

Harold had quite enough of the girl. "There's no need to be rude." He waved his finger at her. "You shouldn't be wandering about the countryside, and not alone with a grown man, and..."

Mydeara rolled her eyes and set about grabbing

trinkets from the goblin's bodies, ignoring Harold completely. Three wildebeests milled nearby, watching them all warily. A ram detached himself from the flock of sheep. He lowered his horns and gave the wildebeests a steely glare. They snorted and then trotted away. He made a note to add fearsome battle sheep to his song.

Harold adjusted his harp on his back. "So where are we off to, good knight?"

Mydeara said, "Bruce, your friends arrived in the village a short while ago. They were asking about you. We should head back to them."

"Oh no, I'm not heading anywhere near those two. I have a quest to be on, and it doesn't involve them."

The girl looked worried. "But I have to go back. I don't want to go back alone."

"You came out here alone, what's the difference? Besides, you're pretty handy with that pan. You're hardly a damsel in need of rescuing." Bruce started down the path.

"What kind of knight leaves a girl alone in the face of danger?" she asked.

Bruce stopped and turned around, "I'm sure you'll be fine."

Mydeara huffed. "Well, I never! And by the way, you scream like a girl!"

Bruce scowled. "Do not." He spun around and started off again with the sheep following behind.

Harold took one look at the tears welling in the

girl's eyes and ran to catch up with Bruce. "You're not going to leave her out here all alone, are you?"

"Here's an idea, 'arold, you take her back to the village. She's a good cook. I'm sure she'd make you something to eat for your help and then you could still talk to the survivors."

"I can't escort her back. I need to write my ballad, and you're my inspiration." Harold scratched at his chin. "If she's a good cook, why don't we take her with us?"

Bruce cocked an eyebrow. "Are you seriously suggesting that I take Mydeara with me on my quest?"

Harold sighed. "I'll be with you, a chaperone of sorts. That would make it proper."

"I suppose so." Bruce pursed his lips and pondered the girl. "Having her tag along would be better than going back to that town and facing the sisters."

"Oh, that sounds like a story! You'll have to regale me with the tale later." Harold waved Mydeara to follow them. "Let's be off then. We've a long journey ahead."

"I need to go home. My father will be worried."

"You can send him a message from the next village. How often do you get the chance to go on a real adventure?" asked Harold. He gestured grandly toward Bruce. "With a real knight on a quest, no less!"

"That *would* beat peeling turnips, I suppose, and

it might make for a good story to tell my children someday. Girls need role models too, you know."

"Sure," Harold said with a condescending smile.

Mydeara fastened the pan to the heavy leather belt that held up her skirt and then followed after Bruce. They walked on until the light began to fade and then stopped to set up a quick camp within the sight of a distant forest.

"Mydeara," Harold said. "I have an extra pair of leggings if you'd like to be free of that skirt. It's not practical for the long walk ahead. Might help you blend in a bit better too, not quite so damsel-in-distress looking."

Her eyes narrowed. "You just don't want people to think that the two of you kidnapped me. If I look like a boy, they'll not give me a second thought."

Bruce shrugged. "Is that a bad thing?"

"No," she admitted. "I suppose not."

"Besides," Bruce said, "If we need to fight again, I'd feel better knowing you were able to defend yourself rather than getting tripped up in a skirt."

"Defend myself? I recall quite well who did the defending back there, mister. It wasn't you!"

Bruce blew a long strand of hair from his face. "I seem to recall using my sword a few times."

"Eventually. And I was the one wearing a skirt."

"Just do it, all right? You'll be happier to be free of all that fabric. Trust me," said Bruce.

Mydeara grabbed the proffered leggings from

Harold and stormed off into the grass. When she returned, she plopped down by the fire with the wadded-up skirt and didn't look at either of them.

"So 'arold," Bruce tossed him a stick of dried meat across the fire, "do you know any good songs?"

Harold's feet ached, and he wanted nothing more than to fill his stomach and then curl up next to the fire. Traveling with a knight proved more strenuous than he'd anticipated. For a man clunking around in plate mail all day, he seemed unaffected by the additional weight.

The sheep milled about, searching out places to bed down. Harold stretched out on his cloak and reached for his harp.

"Yeah 'arold, after all this talk of ballads, I'd like to hear a sample of your work." Mydeara gave him a scathing look across the fire.

These two would have to be won over with his song. The girl for certain. Spiteful one, she was.

"Hold on, let me tune my harp." He sat up and reached for the smooth wood frame. His nimble fingers went about their business, a slight adjustment here and there, a single pluck of a note to test it, while his mind drifted through his repertoire. "How about a tale of love?" Girls liked those.

Mydeara rolled her eyes. "I can scarcely wait."

Bruce held up his hand. "Give the bard a chance. He can't be half bad if he's roaming the countryside. He looks pretty well fed and his clothes are in good condition. And he's alive. If he were truly awful, that wouldn't be the case."

Harold's mouth dropped open. "I *am* right here."

"Yeah, yeah, get on with it then." Mydeara gestured at the harp.

Harold took a drink from his waterskin and then cleared his throat and hummed a few notes along the scales he'd learned as a boy. With his voice properly prepared, he struck the first note.

Once upon a springtime eve,
There was a knight by the name of Steve.
His heart lay broken upon the floor,
After his lover proclaimed her love no more.
Lost in sorrow,
He drank till the morrow.
Deep in his cup,
He waved for a wench to fill it up.
She approached the table with a big grin.
She wasn't thin,
But she was a beautiful lass.
And with each step, she jiggled her big, round—

Bruce clapped his hands over his ears. "Enough already, that's horrible!"

Everyone was a critic. Harold frowned. "I was just getting to the good part."

Mydeara shook her head. "I hate to tell you, but there is no good part about that song. The rhythm of the 'fill up the cup' line is off and," she sighed, "it's just not good. Are you sure you make a living doing this?"

"Indeed, I do. Perhaps the two of you just don't appreciate good music. How about this one then?" He strummed a few more notes as his fingers adjusted to their new positions.

Her eyes were blue as the summer skies above.
Her cheeks, pink as a rose that tells of love.
Lips, full and red parted just so,
And skin soft and white as newly fallen snow.
Hair lush and long like the branches of the willow
As she smiles up at me from my pillow.
I give her a wink and find my sword like a rock
And then she grabs hold of my great big—

A hairy hand slapped down over Harold's, filling the air with the ring of a horribly discordant note. "Really, do you think that is appropriate around the girl?"

Harold wrestled his precious harp away from Bruce's hand. "Sorry, it goes over well in taverns. I just thought—"

"Nevermind. Just put that thing away before you do any more damage with it."

Mydeara's brow furrowed. "I don't get it. What did she grab?"

"Forget 'arold even sang that one. Get to sleep. We

have a lot of walking ahead of us tomorrow." Bruce handed the shivering girl his cloak and laid himself out stiffly on the ground. He set his unsheathed sword by his side. The knight seemed entirely comfortable despite the chill of the night air. Maybe all that fur-like hair was an advantage after all. Mydeara settled her head onto her folded skirt and curled up under Bruce's cloak, looking quite cozy.

Silence fell over their little camp. Harold tucked his harp away in his sack, patting the wood as he did so. "They just don't appreciate you," he whispered.

Tucking his cloak around him, he inched toward the fire. With the animals to alert them to danger and a knight to protect him, he wasn't sure why he felt so apprehensive about falling asleep, but it took several hours of watching the stars cross the sky before his eyes finally closed.

🐉 8 🐉

Jonquil Finds Love

Jonquil stood in the shadows of the forest, her shoulders brushing against the branches of the oak trees. The three humans had come into view across the grassy prairie earlier that morning, but their little legs took the rest of the day to make it to the forest's edge. The one with a harp made a noise that drove her to cover her ears. As they walked closer, the one in armor drew her eye.

Such glorious hair. Quite short for a troll, but certainly with the blood of one to have such a mane on him. And very male, she could smell him from her hiding place. His hearty dirt and sweat smell carried on the breeze. Her heart fluttered as did the tiny wings upon her broad back.

Damned things. Jonquil reached back, attempting to silence the annoying wings that rubbed against the branches and made all sorts of rustling noises. As with the other thousand times she'd tried to grab her wings, her thick arms refused to reach the center of her back. No amount of contorting could bring the prize within their grasp. She gave up and ducked under the branches to hunker down in the underbrush. Maybe if she quit thinking about the beautiful specimen before her, her wings would behave.

Broken branches, pinecones, and rocks dug into her bare knees. Nothing to do about that. It would take the hides of ten deer to make a skirt big enough to cover them. Instead, she had settled for a delicate ruffle of badger and mink to mirror the fashion worn by her father's people. To be born of mixed blood was a curse she wished upon none.

Jonquil pushed the wreath of woodland roses back into place upon her head of coarse black hair. Would he find her attractive? She clasped her mighty hands together and hoped so. After all, he would surely understand her mixed troll and fairy blood, not being a full-blood troll himself.

As they reached the edge of the grass, a flock of sheep emerged to mill about the three travelers.

Her stomach rumbled. Breakfast seemed so long ago, and it had been months since she'd ventured far enough from the forest to eat a sheep. The beasties were tough, but she fondly remembered the taste of them. Jonquil wiped a tendril of sticky saliva from her lips. Their furs would make a lovely winter coat. If she ate all of them, she might even have enough hides for sleeves and a hood. She closed her eyes and smiled, imagining the luxurious warmth of a new coat. Maybe she'd also eat the little humans for pestering the armored one.

Jonquil fondled the wooden club at her side, careful for the iron spikes barbing the last two feet of it. Nothing would bother her beloved. With great resolve, she stood, stretching a moment to loosen her muscles—pulling something while trying to put on a display of interest would just be embarrassing.

She ducked under the branches at the tree line and stepped into the grasslands, her club swinging up to rest on her shoulders. She called out, "I've come to save you!" and ran at them.

The armored one drew his sword. The others scattered, though the girl hung back at a distance with what looked to be a long-handled pan in her hands.

"Don't be afraid." She lumbered closer, coming to a stop before him. "We will eat well tonight."

The little troll man looked up at her with terror plain across his face. Maybe he didn't speak troll. Poor thing. She tried the light trilling of fairy instead. "I've come to claim you as my mate. Don't be afraid."

He backed up a few steps. Good, she'd gotten through to him. With all the other creatures scattered, Jonquil lowered her club, resting the end of it in the grass. Her wings fluttered. Thankfully he couldn't see them, small as they were, they didn't even show above her shoulders. She tugged at her dress to get the maximum effect from her cleavage. The fur-lined straps dug into her shoulders with the readjustment. She bent down to get him a good view of what would soon be his.

A good four heads shorter than her, Jonquil gave some thought to the perils of a shorter mate. How would they make things work between them? She sighed. To hear her mother tell it, size didn't seem to matter. She'd been bathing in the river when she felt something *down there*, but when she looked, she hadn't seen anything. She'd said there was a tickle inside and then nothing. Two seasons later, she'd given birth to Jonquil. Neither of them had ever discovered who her father was, but what he was, was perfectly clear.

"You'll do more than tickle me, won't you?" She picked up the troll man by his shoulder, taking care not to dent his armor as she did so. Stroking his pretty hair, she smiled at its silken texture, much like a rabbit. She held him tight to her chest. His pointy hard boots drove into her thighs. "Oww." She held him back a bit so she could see his face. "That hurts."

His sword twitched about in his hand where she realized she held it pinned by his side. "Oh, I'm sorry, am I hurting you, too?" She readjusted her grip.

Crunch. Snap.

One of the arms of his armor flew through the air, exposing his long silken arm to her view. She nuzzled her face in his long arm hair, luxuriating in his pungent man scent. "You know, we can eat later. How about we head into the woods?"

Thwack! A stinging pain ran up Jonquil's calf. She cried out. *Thwack!* The sting came again.

She set the armored troll down to find the girl attacking with her pan. Jonquil gave a mighty kick, sending the girl flying into the air. There, maybe she would leave her alone to enjoy her new mate.

Jonquil reached for the troll knight. His sword slashed into her arm. She yowled. He slashed again, but this time she stepped back quick enough to avoid his blade. "Why do you wish to hurt me?"

Tears welled in her big round eyes. She wiped at her somewhat bulbous nose. Did he find her ugly? He took another swing. She sobbed and ran off into the forest, her huge feet crushing the underbrush with every thundering step. Why did they all find her unattractive?

She relived the shame of being scorned by the male trolls her age, and then by those twice her age. None of them desired the unique creature she'd been born as. It wasn't her fault. She did the best she could with what her parents had given her. From the waist down she was a perfect female troll. From her rotund behind to her huge hairy feet, there was little

any of them could find fault with. Her belly, hairy as
all the others seemed normal enough, perhaps a bit
thin by troll standards, but hard and full of muscle.
Her breasts, surely none could find fault with those.
It had to be the damned wings and her high-pitched
voice. Maybe that was the problem with the little troll.
He couldn't understand her dialect. She smacked
her forehead. That must be it. It had taken her tribe
years to finally understand what she was saying.
How could she expect this stranger to understand?

Jonquil stopped her rampage through the forest
and turned around to head back through her swath
of destruction. She'd apologize. Yes. Then they would
live a long, happy life together. He was small, she had
wings; they could overcome their setbacks together,
make the best of what they'd been dealt. Her wings
fluttered again. What pretty babies they would have.
She ran faster, her footsteps reverberating through
the trees. She came to the edge of the forest and
burst through.

He was gone. They all were, even the sheep.
Jonquil let out a wail of despair. She'd angered
him. Why had she been so wrapped up in her own
insecurities? Tears rolled down her cheeks.

It would be night soon. Maybe they'd start a fire.
That would make them easy to find. She sat down to
watch the sun set and sniffed the air.

❦ 9 ❦

Letters To J'hal

"You're lucky I came along when I did. That thing would have eaten you alive," J'hal said over his shoulder as he led the travelers away from the troll.

"What was it?" The shaken bard glanced over his shoulder as if he could see through the trees to the grasslands where they'd been attacked.

J'hal kept close to the tree line but never entered the forest. "They don't call it the Forest of Fear for nothing. It looked like some sort of troll. I'm J'hal, by the way."

The knight, with dark hair sticking out of every seam in his armor, slogged along behind J'hal, holding his one bare arm to his chest. "It tried to suffocate me in its cleavage."

"That's Bruce, I'm 'arold, and that's Mydeara," said the bard. "Trolls 'ave cleavage? I'll 'ave to remember that for my ballad."

"I don't know," said Bruce. "Maybe they call it trollage. It doesn't really matter. The point is, the damned thing tried to kill me."

Mydeara smiled smugly. "Yeah, and I saved you."

"I wouldn't call you getting catapulted into tomorrow saving me."

"Fine. I *tried* to save you. Doesn't that at least count for something?" said Mydeara.

Bruce offered her a conciliatory nod. "We should count ourselves fortunate that J'hal knew a quick path through the edge of the forest so we could escape that creature."

Mydeara muttered, "We didn't escape, the creature ran away. As a matter of fact, I'm pretty sure it was crying."

"Don't be silly." The bard chuckled. "Trolls don't cry."

Mydeara turned around and shot him a look. "Is that so? Are you a troll expert now? You didn't even know they had cleavage five minutes ago. Then again, you would have seen it for yourself if you weren't cowering in the grass with the sheep."

"I 'ad to protect my 'arp. Besides Bruce seemed to 'ave it under control."

J'hal shook his head. Odd bunch, this. "So where are you all off to?"

"The Wall of Nok," said the hairy knight.

"Ah, so you need to head to the desert then. I can

take you a short way, but then I must get back home."
Besides, he didn't know how long he could stand the
stink of the hairy man, the outspoken girl, and the
strange-speaking bard. Then there were the sheep.
Something was odd about them.

"It will be night soon. We should put some
distance between us and the forest or we will have
nightmares," said J'hal.

"I've already had one." Bruce kept an eye on the
forest.

J'hal led them through the low hills until they
could no longer see the trees. "That should be far
enough. I don't suppose anyone grabbed some wood
before we left the forest?"

They all looked at him as if he were crazy.

"Never mind. We'll make do. What do you have in
that pack of yours, Bruce?"

"Not you too?" Bruce shrugged the pack off his
armored shoulder. "Go ahead, everyone else seems
to think I spend all my coin to feed the world. Why
should you be any different? Help yourself."

J'hal shrugged and reached into the pack. He
pulled out a crushed wheel of cheese and a squashed
apple. "Let me guess, troll damage?"

Bruce nodded as he sat down in the grass. The
sheep immediately fell in around him, bedding down
and uttering contented sheep noises. After passing
the cheese and another couple bruised apples among
them, 'arold fell asleep and the others followed soon

after.

The first rays of sunlight found J'hal's three bleary-eyed companions rubbing their faces and avoiding each other's eyes. J'hal knew that look. "I'm sorry, I thought we were far enough away from the Forest of Fear."

Bruce hacked at his chest-length beard with a dagger, sawing off the long black hair and tossing handfuls over his shoulder. "Well, you were wrong."

The bard sat hunched over with his harp on his lap. He stroked the wood and sang to himself.

J'hal approached the knight cautiously. "So, I take it you didn't sleep well?"

"What was your first clue?" Bruce held up another handful of shorn hair and tossed it into the grass.

"Did your dream have something to do with hair?"

"You're the sharp one, aren't you?" Bruce started in on the hair that hung over his shoulders. He pulled his locks into a ponytail and sawed at it, giving one of the sheep a wicked glare all the while. "You just shut up."

J'hal looked between the knight and the sheep. Odd didn't even begin to cover it. "Cutting off your hair now will help the dream go away? You must have been growing that for years, why cut it for nothing but a nightmare?"

"If I told you that a troll loved you for your hair... that she kissed you and curled up with you while you slept. That she touched you." He inclined his head downward and looked ready to vomit. "If your head full of hair got caught in the squirrel skull trim of her bodice and you nearly suffocated in her trollage before she panicked, ripped a hunk of your hair out, and then took off... Then would you understand?"

"But it was only a dream."

Bruce cut the last of his hair, leaving a jagged mass to fall just at his shoulders. "It definitely wasn't."

Bruce stormed over to the sheep and put his fist in the ram's face. "I don't care how cold the nights get. Your *gift* of hair goes right now, or I'll do some wool shearing with this sword. You hear me?"

Several of the sheep looked at one another and then the ram stared intently at the knight.

"Does he expect an answer?" J'hal whispered to Mydeara.

She waved her hand in the air. "Don't mind them."

He didn't know if he could do that, but he made an effort to try. "What did you dream about?" he asked her.

The girl snapped her gaze away from the knight. "That my village was overrun by goblins."

"I don't think those goblins are going back there," assured Bruce.

"I hope not. Neither of us is nearby to do anything about it if they do."

J'hal left the girl to her sour spirits and walked toward the bard. He tripped. Getting to his feet, he noticed a large indent in the dirt. It appeared to be in the shape of a huge club. And as he looked even closer, all the grass and leaves to one side of Bruce were crushed as if something large and heavy had lain in them during the night. He didn't recall hearing anything. The animals hadn't made a sound. Maybe the ground had been that way before they came to this spot. It had been dusk, after all, when they stopped. He shrugged and went to the bard's side.

'arold tucked his harp away in his pack and looked up. "What?"

"What did you dream?"

"That I played before the king and queen of Gambreland with a court full of lords and ladies in attendance. They all sat quiet, listening to my every note."

That didn't sound so nightmarish. "And?"

"And every note was off, and they broke out into laughter and jeered at my words."

"Hmm, yes, that doesn't sound pleasant."

"But realistic," muttered Mydeara. "So J'hal, what did you dream about?"

"Seeing Gambreland torn apart by war. My beautiful country ran red with blood, and lightning brought down fire from the skies."

Bruce got to his feet and shuddered as he skirted the indent on the ground. "We should get moving. I don't want to spend another night near that forest as long as I live."

The others nodded. J'hal led them deeper into the hills which slowly transformed into a rolling plain surrounding a wide stretch of water.

As they drew closer, Bruce scowled. "What is that? The River of Ruin?"

"Don't be silly," J'hal snickered. "It's just a river."

"Are you sure?"

"Quite. I've lived here all my life. We'll be passing through the capital in an hour or two. If you'd like, we can stop at my farm and get a good warm meal."

"Sounds lovely," Mydeara let out a wistful sigh.

٭

When the fields of wheat came into view, J'hal could barely hold back his urge to run. "Come on! We're almost there." He danced in place, hopping from foot to foot. He could already taste his mother's fresh bread and her rabbit stew. The thought of a mug of mead made his mouth water.

The house stood just as it had when he'd left it. Logs stacked high upon a foundation of head-sized stones. Except the front door hung open. Mother would never stand for that.

And where were the cows? Even the chickens were silent. He stopped in his tracks. "'arold, why don't you stay here with the animals? I'd like to borrow Bruce and Mydeara for a moment. We should be right back."

"Don't be too long, I'm hungry too." 'arold sat down at the edge of the wheat field.

Bruce glanced at the sheep. They hung back with the bard, rather than following the knight as they usually seemed to do.

J'hal sidled up to the knight. "You wouldn't happen to have an extra dagger on you?"

The knight fished around in his pack. "You'll give it back, right?"

"Of course."

"Good. I like this one." Bruce handed J'hal a dagger with a bone grip. "Be good to it."

J'hal examined the hand-length blade. "Just how does one *be good* to a knife? You mean, kill with it? Kill a lot with it? Don't get blood on it? Don't sink it into hardwoods? If you're going to imply how I should care for something that I'm borrowing, please be explicit so I don't have you threatening to kill me with it later."

"No on the hardwoods and no stone. Clean it before giving it back and don't lose it. I just bought the thing before we left for this cursed country."

"Got it. Mydeara, do you have your pan ready?"

"Yes."

The three of them set off into the yard. Footprints showed signs of a scuffle as they approached the house.

J'hal's heart plummeted into his stomach. Something was wrong. With Bruce and Mydeara right behind him, he ran for the house.

He burst inside to find it empty.

The bench beside the table lay on its side. The bowl Mother liked to keep full of fruit was on the floor, the contents lay scattered under the table. The shelf that hung on the wall was askew, as was the portrait of his family that had been drawn by a traveling artist at the summer festival when he was a child. Father had paid good coin for that.

"Someone got roughed up here," said Bruce. "No blood though. I suppose that's a good sign."

Mydeara nodded. "This is your family?" she asked, pointing to the portrait.

J'hal nodded proudly. His tall, fair-haired parents smiled at him from the parchment, their hands resting on his shoulders as he stood between them.

"So, you're adopted then?" she asked.

"No. Why do you ask?"

"Pointy ears, other-worldly good looks, tall, slender." Mydeara gave him a quick once over from head to foot. "They're elves. You, my burly, farmish friend, have hair as black as night, muscles all over by the looks of it, ears like the rest of us, and are significantly shorter than these people you call your parents. I think it's safe to assume you're adopted."

"They...I don't know. I never thought about it before. What does it matter?"

Mydeara looked to Bruce like they used some

unspoken language he didn't know.

"Not the most observant one, are you?" said Bruce, shaking his head. "Never mind, let's take a look around and see if anything is missing."

Bruce walked out the door and clanked across the yard, beckoning J'hal to follow him. "We need to figure out who did this so we can maybe get your parents back."

"Maybe?" The thought of his parents being gone forever brought on a cold panic.

Bruce gave him a strained smile. "I'm sure they're fine. Come on."

J'hal followed Bruce to the barn, taking inventory in his head. Nothing seemed out of place. The cows were all inside as if the attack had happened early enough in the morning that his father never got the chance to let them out for the day. "Just the chickens seem to be missing."

Bruce slowly started back toward the house. "How many were there?"

"Eight."

"Hmm, easy enough to stuff in a sack, I suppose. From their tracks, I'd say there were at least five men." He gazed out at the field where 'arold sat. The sheep milled around him, happily chewing on grass. "Let's get Mydeara and see about following those tracks.

Inside the house, Mydeara stood near the table, picking up canisters that had fallen from the shelf.

"Put those down," said J'hal.

"I'm just looking around. I'm not hurting anything." Mydeara shook her head. "Unlike what your visitors did." She nodded toward a small wooden chest on the floor. "There's a note daggered to the top."

"Daggered?"

She let out an exasperated sigh, strode over to the chest, picked it up, and set it on the table. A very plain scratched up dagger had been plunged through a scrap of paper and into the top of the chest.

"Oh. I'm not to touch that chest. Father said so," J'hal said. "The dagger wasn't there before."

Mydeara looked to the ceiling and shook her head. She pulled the note free. "Seems your parents owed taxes to some overlord with a seriously long name." She held out the note to him. "Killing them seems a bit extreme," said Bruce. "Hard to maintain a tax base when your subjects are dead. They've probably been taken as slaves."

'arold crept in. "Find anything useful?"

"Maybe." Bruce beckoned him over.

J'hal studied the note. "An overlord took over the country before I was born. He's kind of evil."

"I'd say so." She pondered the chest, running her hands over the smooth wooden surface. "What's in here?"

Curious, he'd peeked once as a child when his parents were outside. He'd been expecting treasure but had been sorely disappointed. "Nothing, it's empty."

Mydeara flipped the lid open and ran her fingers over the inside too. Something clicked. She grinned and held up a folded packet of paper. "Doesn't look empty to me."

"What?" He peered over her shoulder.

"Apparently you're not very good at snooping. There was a hidden compartment." She pulled a faded red ribbon from the thick sheet of folded parchment. A wax stamp imprinted with a crown adorned the top. "Looks important."

It did. J'hal righted the bench and sat down with the sealed parchment in hand.

Bruce and 'arold huddled in closer, looming over him.

"Well, open it," Bruce said, waving at the paper.

The packet sat heavy in his hands. Dust covered the royal-looking seal. He blew on it, making himself sneeze. He glanced up to see everyone waiting. J'hal bit his lip and then cracked the seal. A faint sound, like a whisper, seemed to come from the wax as it crumbled into a hundred fragments that fell to the floor. He unfolded the paper with care.

Inside, heavily flourished strokes of black ink formed letters. As his eyes strained to make sense of all the curlicues and squiggles, they became words and words drew into sentences. And the sentences proclaimed the babe that accompanied the letter the rightful ruler of Gambreland.

"I should be the king?" The word *king* sounded strange on his lips.

"Give me that." Mydeara snatched the letter out of his hand. Her mouth moved as she read. "You've got to be kidding."

Bruce scowled. "You're not the king of anything yet. Not unless you have a plan to get rid of whoever is doing the ruling at the moment."

'arold clapped and grinned. "This is all so exciting! I will 'ave to write a ballad about this too."

"I thought you were busy writing one about me?" Bruce glared at him out of the corner of his eye.

"I will. Don't worry. But it's not every day that I get to sing the tale of a king fighting for his throne."

"Oh please," Mydeara exclaimed. "Every third song a bard sings is about a mighty king fighting for his throne. The others are about knights fighting for their king or inflated feats intended to make women swoon for a knight or a king."

J'hal took the parchment from Mydeara, folded it, and slipped it into his pocket. "You'll all come with me, right? I may need a little help with this 'fighting for my throne' thing."

Mydeara glanced at Bruce.

He sighed. "I'm on a quest already."

"If you'll help me take the throne, I'll see that you are well rewarded."

The bard piped up, "Think of all the heroic deeds

this could add to your ballad."

"Fine." Bruce sighed. "What's one more side quest?"

J'hal grinned. "That's settled then. How about a night's rest before we head out?"

Bruce took J'hal's parents' bed. He took off his armor, setting the pieces on the floor with metallic clanks. He let out a hearty exhale and dropped onto the bed. It groaned. "Damn that feels good."

'arold's head perked up. "You wear that heavy stuff all the time? I thought you just didn't feel safe taking it off when we were sleeping outside."

"Nope. Part of knight training. You've got to be able to wear your plate with pride. We spent months working up our stamina to pass that test."

An odor, long contained within the metal, wafted through the room. Mydeara got up and opened all the windows. Even with the threat of someone finding him there, J'hal didn't stop her.

'arold cleared his throat. "'ow about I sing us a song to put us all to sleep?"

"Shouldn't be hard," Bruce muttered not quite under his breath.

Anxious to hear the song of a true bard, J'hal laid back and closed his eyes to better concentrate on the first soft notes from the bard's harp.

Back in the day when dragons flew free
Before the age of man 'ad yet to come

The winged ones were ruled by one called Gee
'is eyes were cloudy and 'is tail was numb
But most wise was 'e, this dragon Gee

'e led 'is kind across mountains and streams
Through the sky they flew from morn til night
Til they came to a land ruled by the female, Meems
The two leaders clashed in a mighty fight
But most wise was she, this dragon Meems

She pinned the great dragon down to the ground
Gee swore, 'e writhed, 'e snapped and 'e bucked
She whispered in 'is ear and 'e flipped her round
Meems gave him a wink and a grin. Then they...

J'hal woke the next morning wondering how the tale of the dragons had ended. 'arold lay slumped down in his chair with his harp still in his lap. Somehow, he'd expected more from a bard. His farmer father had had a better sense of rhythm.

Pleasant smells reached his nose. He and the others rose from their blankets and came to the table. Mydeara bustled about with his mother's apron tied about her waist.

"Go on and eat. I already did. Like I was going to wait for you lazy lot to get up."

J'hal sat down and set heartily into his breakfast. "My mother always waited to eat until we men were finished. I thought all women did the same?"

Mydeara's eyes narrowed. "I cooked the food. I'll eat whenever I please, thank you very much."

J'hal shoved a mouthful of hotcakes in before she reached for her pan.

Bruce clanked into the kitchen, back in full armor, but his hair hung in mangy-looking clumps. He ran his hand through it and came away with a thready glob that he dropped on the floor.

"Are you...shedding?" Mydeara asked.

Bruce grinned. "Yes. It seems the sheep don't trust my shearing abilities." Then he turned to J'hal. "Gather all the supplies you can carry. We're going to see about putting you on the throne."

Mydeara leaned close to Bruce, handing him a plate. "Is that a good idea? He's an idiot," she said not very under her breath while glancing at J'hal.

Bruce glanced at J'hal over his shoulder and whispered equally as loudly, "Yes, but he'll be a grateful idiot."

⚔ 10 ⚔

Sneaky Ed

Ed stood behind the copse of trees, observing the four men and their barnyard's worth of animals coming down the road. They'd be around the curve any minute.

He rubbed a hand over his face, making sure everything was as it should be, straightened his stained robes, and then smeared just a little more dirt on his hands for effect. Grabbing his walking stick, he stepped out into the road and tried out his chosen gait.

"Ho there," a voice called out.

Ed smiled to himself and then promptly returned his expression to dour before turning around. "Oh hello." Sheep, cattle? He took in all the animals now milling around him. "Quite a farm you have traveling with you."

"I didn't have anyone to take care of them at the farm, so the cows had to come with," said a muscular young man with dark hair and eyes.

Where are you headed?" Ed asked.

"The capital," said a short man wearing a jaunty green cap. From the harp peeking out of his pack, Ed figured he must be the typical bard type.

"I see. I happen to be going there myself. Would you mind keeping an old man company on the road?"

The brawny lad nodded and looked to a knight. "What do you say, Bruce?"

The knight threw up his hands. "Fine. What's one more?"

It seemed the knight was in charge of this motley band of travelers. Ed stroked his chin, belatedly remembering his well-manicured goatee was absent. "You wouldn't happen to be on a quest, would you?"

The bard grinned. "Oh yes! And quite a quest indeed. See, J'hal here just learned he's the rightful king of Gambreland."

Ed strangled his walking stick. "A king, you say? Well, isn't that interesting." He shuffled along as if he couldn't care less, but on the inside, he fumed.

Damn, the seer was right.

Ed had followed all the instructions for a successful takeover—put the current regime to death, ruled the country with an iron fist, built up storehouses of gold and silver. He'd practiced evil to the best of his abilities. He'd even gone the extra step of selling his soul as insurance on his endless reign. Yet, within the first year, a seer had arrived at his castle door with an urgent message from the netherworld. He recalled the conversation in vivid detail.

The seer, dressed in robes near as fine as his own, though rather than black, the seer opted for a cheery yellow. Ed had cringed at the mere sight of them. The man had asked for a coin, holding out his hand until a silver disc rested on his palm.

"Let's hear it then."

The seer nodded and adopted a far-off look as he spoke.

> *The son lives.*
> *Hidden though he be,*
> *He'll overthrow you with the number thirty-three.*

"Enough of this nonsense. If you have something definite to say, spit it out."

The seer scowled. "You take all the shine off the silver, you know that?"

"Yes, yes." He waved the man on. "It comes with being evil. Speak plainly, or you'll end up in my dungeon."

"The boy will be rounding the curve on Miller's road at noon seventeen years and two hundred and three days from now."

"Thank you, that's much better. Now, could you

please explain how the infant son of the royal family survived when I saw them all put to death with my own eyes?"

The seer shrugged. "Maybe you should have done the job yourself. A task so important as that—"

"I *did* do it myself. Are you deaf? I said, I put them to death with my own eyes. I offered up my little toe to the Ninth Darkness for 'the look that kills'." He focused on the seer, giving him a little taste of what the look could do.

The seer squirmed in his sunny robes, his eyes growing wide. He backed away. "That's all I know. Honest."

"We'll see about that." He waved for his minions to take the seer to the dungeon. They'd worked on him for a week, but the man yielded up nothing more. Then, due to rampant problems with dungeon overcrowding, he'd had to let the seer go. No need to invite bad karma by killing one of the mouths of the gods.

And here the boy was, just as promised.

"J'hal is it?"

The young man nodded, his dark eyes alight with eagerness.

"Wish to be king, do you?"

"I hadn't given it much thought until yesterday when the overlord's tax collectors took my parents away while I was gone. We found a letter hidden in the same chest the tax collectors' note had been left on that explained my birthright. Like a gift from the gods, you know? I would have likely never found the hidden note if it weren't for the tax collectors."

Ed managed a pained smile. A gift from the gods indeed. If he ever got a moment with those gods, they were going to hear out all his complaints. There were a lot of them.

Chiseled muscles, strong jaw, rugged dark features. J'hal didn't resemble the previous royal family at all. "Your parents were taken, you said?"

The young man nodded. "From our farm out near the Forest of Fear."

"Was anything, err, *stolen* from your farm when your parents were taken?" Ed asked.

"Our chickens."

"Ah, yes. Interest on those back taxes. The overlord is quite stringent with his collection policies."

Bruce strode up next to Ed. "This overlord, what's his name?"

"Surely you've heard of him?" Ed turned to survey the group.

J'hal shrugged, as did the rest of them.

"It was written on the tax notice, but the penmanship was so awful, I couldn't read it," said the girl.

Ed's blood began to boil. What did he pay his publicity minions for? This man lived a day out of the capital and had never heard of him? His people scrawled his name so badly, it couldn't be read? He scowled. If word wasn't getting out around his own country, that explained the lack of heroes trying to overthrow him. How was he supposed to uphold his evil rating if there weren't any threats? No wonder the entire country had sunk into a pleasant place to live despite all his evil efforts.

Did he have to do everything himself?

"His name is Darkious Maximus, Evil Overlord Extraordinaire and Master of the Nine Darknesses. Does that ring any bells?"

They all shrugged, but he swore he caught one of the sheep glaring at him. "Nothing? Really?"

They shook their heads.

"Not even a rumor?"

J'hal shrugged. "Sorry, no. Is he quite evil?"

Ed's voice rose. "Well, yeah. Hence the name."

J'hal looked worried. "Oh, no. He's got my parents."

Bruce said, "Don't put too much stock in the name, boy. It could be misleading like those big men that get names like Tiny or Slim."

Ed clenched his teeth. How could his staff have failed so miserably? He wanted to kill someone. Best not to do that quite yet though. These adventurers were the best thing he could ask for. He needed to make a spectacle of defeating them to boost his evil rating, and to get his name out there to draw more heroes in. Doing away with them quietly would do him no good at all. Besides, there were only four of them, far short of the prophesized thirty-three. If he saw them gathering more support, he'd kill them quickly.

They walked along for a few hours, exchanging small talk until the bard with the horrible accent made an announcement.

"I've come up with a little song about this Evil Overlord. Would you all like to 'ear it?"

Ed gritted his teeth. If there was one thing he couldn't stand, it was disrespect. "That's Darkious Maximus, Evil Overlord Extraordinaire and Master of the Nine Darknesses."

"Right. 'im. Would you like to 'ear it?" The bard plucked a few hopeful notes on his harp as they walked.

His very own ode to evil. Ed closed his eyes and smiled. How long had it been since anyone had made up a song about him? Oh, that's right, he scowled, never. "I would love to hear your song."

The others all groaned. He couldn't imagine why.

Evil Overlord, they call 'im
In these lands 'ere abouts
'e wears black clothes, gives dark looks

Assumptions were just under disrespect on his list of annoyances. "I don't mean to interrupt, but have you seen Darkious Maximus, Evil Overlord Extraordinaire and Master of the Nine Darknesses before?"

Harold's fingers froze over the strings. "Umm, no. Why?"

"Then how do you know what he wears?"

Harold scratched the back of his neck. "I just guessed. Seems to me, most followers of the evil sort favor black. Kind of standard, if you know what I mean."

Standard? He was standard? Ed fumed. "I see. Carry on." As the bard found his place on the strings, Ed made a mental note to have his wardrobe minions find another color for him to wear. Maybe a nice dark violet or midnight blue. Something, anything, less...standard.

and when 'e's displeased 'e shouts
The maidens, they tremble
The men, they quake
And 'eros come forth, 'is life to take.

Maidens trembling sounded quite nice. Ed's grip eased on his staff. "One more thing. These heroes, do you think it would be so easy for them to defeat Darkious Maximus, Evil Overlord Extraordinaire and Master of the Nine Darknesses?"

Harold struck a note more off than the rest. "Never know. Depends on 'ow wrapped up in 'is evil 'e is. That sort is often so consumed in some evil scheme they end up completely blind to an attack the rest of us could see a country away." He rapped his knuckles on his head. "Not the brightest bunch, those evil ones. Usually, the ones not loved by their mommies, maybe daddy ran over the beloved pet with his haycart, bad grades in school, or they hung out with the wrong crowd. That sort of thing."

Ed's mouth hung open. When he finally gathered the wherewithal to close it, he sputtered, "That's not how it is at all, I'll have you know."

Bruce gave him an odd look. "You some sort of expert on Evil Overlords, Ed?"

"No, no, nothing like that." Ed gritted his teeth and continued on his way. "Just seems like with a man so evil as Darkious Maximus, Evil Overlord Extraordinaire and Master of the Nine Darknesses, would be carved of deeper stuff than your typical evil overlord material."

The girl piped up, "He must be pretty evil then."

Ed decided right then that he liked her. "To be sure."

Harold cleared his throat and struck a chord.

'e calls down demons and snakes from the sky
kill a man 'e can with a look from 'is eye.

Maybe word had traveled after all. At least 'arold seemed to know about the evil eye.

But when the 'ero comes about

The overlord will shake and shout
To no avail, his efforts will come to pass
For the 'ero will kick 'is boney—

Ed's voice came out shrill, "Say, is anyone else hungry?"

"We just ate, old man." Bruce shook his head. "We've got to keep moving or it will be late in the afternoon tomorrow before we make it to the capital. I imagine J'hal here is a little anxious for his big meeting with this Evil Overlord."

J'hal paled. "Wait, I've got to meet Darkious Maximus, Evil Overlord Extraordinaire and Master of the Nine Darknesses? I have to figure out how to get my parents back from the evil overlord? I thought I was going to deal with the current king."

Bruce rolled his eyes. "That *is* the current king, you lout. You really have lived your whole life on a farm." He shook his head. "Never studied the ruling class, have you? See, it comes down to a couple of things. Royal families, kings and queens and the like, or evil overlords. Sometimes there's the odd conniving uncle playing regent for a naïve princess, but to be honest, that lot is just a lower class of evil overlord."

Ed raised his wrinkled hand. "Now you just hold on there. Unless those uncles earned their place by gaining a suitable evil rating, they belong to the royalty side."

The girl's brow furrowed. "What is this evil rating? How high would an uncle have to get?"

Knowing too much information would raise even more suspicion, Ed sighed. "On a scale of six to six hundred sixty-six, they'd have to be a two hundred, I think. I'm not really sure. It's just something an old man overhears." He shrugged.

"Mydeara," Bruce said, "why don't you go check on the sheep and cattle?"

Bruce waited until the girl had fallen back. "So, Ed, tell it to me straight, what kind of chance do you think I'd have against this Darkious Maximus, Evil Overlord Extraordinaire and Master of the Nine Darknesses?"

Ed looked him over. An oddly hairy fellow, he was. Hair seemed to slough off him in the gentle breeze. Did humans shed like dogs? The knight was missing one sleeve of his armor but the rest of him appeared to be in good shape. A bent and dinged-up sword hung by his side and even traipsing around all day in plate armor didn't seem to slow the man. "Depends, I suppose. Are any of your weapons magic?"

J'hal cast Bruce a hopeful glance. Bruce shook his head.

"Magic armor?" Ed asked.

"Nope."

"Well, that will lower your chances by far. Hmm. Know any spells?"

Bruce shook his head.

"Are you of mysterious parentage?"

"My father was a cooper, and my mother baked a wicked apple pie. She won a few contests," he said proudly.

"Doesn't really qualify, I'd say." Ed tapped his chin. How often did he have a chance to get the rundown on the competition? Couldn't be luckier, he figured. "Has anyone ever uttered the phrase, 'you are *the one*' to you or about you, to your knowledge?"

Bruce walked along in silence for a long moment. "Only this one boy when I was a kid, he thought I'd stolen his boots, and he was making threatening gestures at me from the other side of the classroom. He only mouthed the words. Does that count?"

"No, sorry." Near cackling with evil glee, Ed took a deep breath to calm himself. "I'd say you have as good of a chance as the next hero." Which was none. The evil glee threatened to burst forth again. He masked it with a sputtering cough.

Late evening brought them within sight of the capital. Ed smiled to see his familiar black towers set against the dusky sky. While the night view always brought him a sense of calm and rightness with the world, it was the daytime view that took a first-time visitor's breath away.

"We should camp here. We will reach the gates by late morning if we get an early start."

The others agreed and they settled down for the night.

❦ 11 ❦

Timininious Is Evil

Timininious adjusted his wizard's robes. It wouldn't do to come into the presence of Darkious Maximus, Evil Overlord Extraordinaire and Master of the Nine Darknesses looking shabby and ripe from the road. There was a protocol to follow between users of magic. Offending the overlord wasn't the impression he wanted to make.

He addressed the minion standing outside the door. "When will he see me?"

"He'll see your head on a spike if you don't quit pestering me, old man. Return to your seat."

Timininious huffed. It was hard to find good minions these days, he understood that, but there was no need for rudeness. He returned to the wooden bench inlaid with broken glass and shifted in place until he found a spot that offered minimal poking. If this bench cut his new robes, Timininious fumed, he'd submit a request for reimbursement. That would get the minions all riled up for sure. No one liked additional paperwork.

Minions came and went. All wearing their black uniforms: black leggings, fitted black shirt emblazoned with a silver DM just over their hearts, and black boots. They wore their hair bound back as per the employee manual, clean, free of lice—at least he didn't notice any of them itching their scalp—and dyed black, a free perk Timininious planned to make use of if he were lucky enough to get hired. His grey hairs needed help, and the forces of good just didn't offer anything in the way of benefits in that direction. They embraced their whites and grays.

Timininious was sick of being called *old man.* How fortunate that he'd seen the minions wanted ad while at the herbalist.

A minion passed by, dusting the wall plaques as she traveled down the hall. The one he'd stared at for an hour read: Ye Evil Antechamber. The script, with its imposing heavy strokes, boded good—in an evil sort of way—things about the man within. Dust drifted through the air. Timininious, without thinking, uttered a quick spell to prevent sneezing.

Golden glitter showered him, dusting his robes and hair. He groaned. Would he ever rid himself of this curse on his magic that made all his spells go wrong? He looked up at the otherworldly mist hovering just out of his reach. A piece of glitter lodged itself in his eye. He swore.

Ever since he'd taken the job to steal a huge crystal known as the God's Eye from the great dragon Jaskernect's cave of treasure, his magic had been off. Damned dragons and their curses. He'd meant to cast a spell to lift the fabled treasure from the sleeping dragon's grasp and transport the treasure outside the cave where he could safely escape with it and make a fortune. The crystal had no sooner risen from the sleeping dragon's grasp when it blinked out of existence. He had no idea where the thing went.

Without the treasure to exchange for his fortune, he now had to find a job. And figure out how to keep it with his magic going awry. Timininious sighed.

Small spells, he repeated to himself. Small stuff that couldn't go too wrong. Maybe if he could get in good with the evil overlord, he could offer some suggestions on getting rid of the dragon's curse. After all, who had more knowledge of curses than an evil overlord?

"Sir?" A female voice said. "They are ready for you inside."

With his eye watering and likely bloodshot from his efforts to dislodge the glitter, Timininious rose from the glass shards and shook the golden flecks from his robes.

The woman frowned at the mess he left on the black stone. "That's not going to gain you any favor with the cleaning minions."

"I'm sorry, I don't have anything with me to clean it up."

"Oh please. You might as well leave already. Apologizing." She snorted and consulted the parchment in her hand. "You did check off evil on your application. Are you sure you answered that truthfully?"

"Yes, of course."

She shook her head. "If you say so. I have a feeling I'm going to be hearing about this interview later." She headed toward the door and mumbled, "like when we're all sitting around the cauldron, boiling up some kitten heads in babies' tears, drinking our tankards of chilled blood and laughing."

"Don't you mean cackling?" He distinctly remembered the 'no laughing' clause in the handbook.

She turned around and grinned. "There might be hope for you after all."

Though he knew it would be better if he didn't question, he couldn't help but ask, "You don't really eat the kitten heads, do you?"

"Would it be a problem if we did?"

"No, I suppose not." Bile rose in his throat. He swallowed it down.

"Good, because they're so tasty with a crisp salad topped with bunny eyes."

Timininious gagged, but he followed her through

the doorway.

Three tables were set up within the room. Two men and a woman sat at each one with a long line of applicants trailing to each of them.

"What is all this?" He'd not seen anyone else enter during his entire wait.

"Open audition day. Don't tell me you didn't see the banner outside?"

He shrugged. "Must have missed it."

"I'll have to have a word with the publicity minions. Their job performance rating has been on the decline for months." She scribbled a note on the parchment in her hands.

"Hey, Rian." One of the men at the nearest table waved to her.

"My boyfriend," she mouthed over her shoulder to Timininious. She waved back.

"Is that the guy that filled out an application when we had open auditions?"

"Yeah." She held up the parchment.

"We'll take him, no reason he should have to wait." He winked at Rian.

"Right." Rian handed him the application and turned back to Timininious. "Malforus will take good care of you. Best of luck." She backed away from them.

Malforus gazed at him with narrow, dark eyes. "So, you think you have what it takes to be evil?"

Timininious stood up straight. "Yes, I do."

"Good for you. Now, get in line."

"But—"

Everyone in the line snickered.

Malforus tossed the parchment aside and turned his attention to the woman next in line. "So, you think you have what it takes to be evil?"

The petite girl stepped forward and grinned, showing off two deep dimples beside her plump, pink lips. "I do, but don't you get sick of saying that? That's got to be very tiring. Is it required? Maybe you could ask about switching it up a little to keep things interesting?"

"Switching things up a little?" Malforus scoffed. "We don't do that here. We follow directions. Perhaps you can't read? It's the name of the event. Didn't you see the banner?"

She blushed. "I'm so sorry. I didn't see a banner."

"Damn publicity people." He turned to the woman beside him. "Get one of them up here. Right now!"

She nodded and dashed off.

The applicant played with a tangle of her long black hair, blinking slowly. "So what do I do?"

Malforus glanced at his remaining cohort. The other man nodded toward a door on the side of the room.

"What was your name?" Malforus asked.

"Cindy?"

"It's your lucky day, Cindy. While you *are* super cute, we don't do that here either. And sadly, you're not quite evil enough to make up for it. However, we do have some lovely parting gifts for you. If you'll just go through the door over there, someone will help you."

Cindy's bright smile collapsed and her dimples vanished. Her head hung low as she made her way to the door.

Malforus looked up at the line. "Next."

A young man stepped in front of the table.

"So, you think you have what it takes to be evil?"

A shrill scream sounded from behind the door Cindy had gone through. The judges exchanged a look of amusement.

"Yes." The applicant said, giving them both an annoyed look.

Malforus held up a hand. "One moment, we need a full panel of judges."

The female judge returned along with a dour dwarf. "He's been nominated by the publicity minions to speak on their behalf."

Malforus addressed the dwarf. "This banner your people spent so much time and coin on, why does no one notice it?"

"Are you kidding? We worked for days on that damn thing!" He slammed his meaty fists onto his hips and glared at Malforus.

"Where is this banner?"

"Right on the front of the keep." The dwarf glared at the line of applicants. "You're all blind!"

"Let's take a break for a moment and go outside to evaluate the issue." Malforus started out of the room with the dwarf. "You, wizard, come with us. Since you walked right by it too, maybe you can help explain why you missed it."

Timininious took off after them. They walked quickly, their hard-soled boots echoing off the stone walls with a deep ominous sound. He had to almost run to keep up, but his footsteps didn't sound nearly as impressive.

They passed under the wicked-looking spiked gate that was held half open by a chain attached to a winch on the wall beside the main entrance. Once in the courtyard, Timininious took a deep breath of the fresh air. The air inside had smelled distinctly like brimstone, more so the deeper he'd gone in.

Malforus turned in a slow circle. "So, where is this monumental banner?"

"Right there." The dwarf pointed to the flat front face of the black keep.

Timininious glanced up, tilting his head from side to side in an attempt to make out what he was pointing at. "It's just a bunch of bones. I thought they were decorations."

The dwarf's shoulders slumped. "How were we to know that the crows would clean them off so quickly? Do you have any idea the amount of time that went into attaching all those corpses to the keep? Those walls are high, I'll have you know. And making the words out of bodies isn't an easy task. They get ripe pretty quick. I thought dotting the I's with the heads was a nice touch. Kind of loses the effect without the actual eyes in place though." He kicked at a stone underfoot.

Malforus shook his head. "Would it kill you people to get a message out in a logical and legible manner? It's a good thing I suggested flyers be placed in town or we'd all be bored stiff today."

"We'll keep that in mind for next time." The dwarf reached up to jab his thick finger into Malforus's chest. "Maybe, if you have a helpful idea, you should bother to show up for the planning meetings."

Malforus quirked a black eyebrow and stroked his standard black goatee. "You should remember, I'm third in command while Darkious Maximus, Evil Overlord Extraordinaire and Master of the Nine Darknesses is out of the office."

The dwarf pulled his hand back and sneered. "And when he comes back, you'll be fourth—a nothing, like the rest of us."

A most evil smile crept across Malforus's thin lips. "True. But today. I'm third." He clapped his hands twice.

Two armed minions leapt from the shadows of the keep and stood at attention.

Malforus pointed at the dwarf. "Take him to the dungeon. Give him the full employee tour."

One of the armed men cleared his throat. "Excuse

me, sir, I'll need to see proof of your current status."

"Yes, of course." He rummaged around in his pockets. "I have that here somewhere."

The dwarf snickered. "Nothing. Nothing. Nothing. They don't even know your face."

Malforus whipped out a palm-length roll of parchment and unrolled it. A red stamp of DMEOEMND adorned the bottom half while two rows of neat script filled the top.

The guard minion read it and nodded. "Yes, sir."

"On second thought, give him the deluxe tour. I think he's earned it," said Malforus.

"They'll be happy for a quality visitor. The dungeons have been a bit quiet since the publicity minions used up the majority of the entertainment."

Malforus pointed to the bones. "Did you notice what they did with them?"

The guards looked up. "What's that supposed to be?"

The dwarf stomped his feet. "Doesn't anyone appreciate art anymore?"

Timininious did his best to be unobtrusive. No question about it, Malforus had a high evil rating. The guards each grabbed one of the little man's arms and picked him up, swinging him between them as they walked back inside.

"Let's get back to work, shall we?" Malforus shooed Timininious toward the keep.

They crossed back under the gleaming points

of the gate and through an arch of mummified heads. Candles, set in the skull sconces along the halls, flickered as they traveled back to the room where he had waited for hours and then into the Evil Antechamber. The line and the same applicant were right where they had been as if frozen in time. Murmurs from the other two tables off in the distance barely registered in his ears. Timininious took his place at the end of the line.

Malforus sat behind the table. "There, now that matter is settled. Where were we?"

"He was about to state his name," the female judge said, nodding to the man at the front of the line.

"Rex."

"All right, Rex. So what evil are you going to do for us today?"

Rex smiled, baring pointed teeth. "This." He turned around and sunk his teeth into the neck of the man in line behind him. Blood spurted across the next two people in line. A murmur passed through the other applicants. Rex spat out a mouthful of flesh and turned back to the judges. Behind him, the gnawed-on man collapsed onto the floor, clasping his hand over the gushing wound.

The other male judge stood and yelled, "Clean up at table one."

Within a minute, three minions arrived. One got to work with a bucket of water and a cloth while the other two carried the wounded man away.

Malforus nodded. "Rex, you have my vote to pass, but you'll need another vote to get to the next round. What do you say, guys?"

The woman picked at her blood-red fingernails and shrugged. "I've seen it before. Not very original."

The other judge pursed his lips and templed his fingers under his chin. "Well Rex, here's the thing. You might not be too original, but you took a chance. You've got moxie. I like moxie. You've got my vote. But keep in mind, we're going to have to see something just a bit more impressive in the future."

Rex nodded. "I'll do my best. Thank you."

Malforus sighed. "Don't get all polite on us now. Remember, we're evil. Think evil."

"Will do," said Rex.

"Through the door at the back of the room." Malforus pointed over his shoulder. "Next."

The line shuffled forward over the next three hours. The cleanup minions came and went several more times. The occasional scream from the side door roused him back to alertness as did the few applicants that ran bawling and retching from the room.

As if they'd never witnessed evil before. Amateurs.

"Next."

Timininious found himself facing the table.

"Oh, it's you again." Malforus rubbed his face and blinked his sagging eyes. "We don't get many wizards looking for hire. You sort usually branch out into your own overlord status. Why are you here?"

He'd been dreading this question. Admitting he was cursed and hoping for help to find the cure didn't seem like a good selling point. He went with a less negative answer. "I'm not good with self-management. I need structure." He saw the woman write 'not a self-starter' on his application.

"So," Malforus said in a tired voice as he glanced at the parchment, "Timininious, do you think you have what it takes to be evil?"

"I like to think so."

"And what evil will you be doing for us today?" asked the woman.

Timininious did his best to keep his grimace to himself. *Please work. Please work.* He pulled one of the most simple beginner spells from his memory.

"I will strike someone down with lightning. Your choice, as long as it isn't me."

The woman grinned. "Wise man."

Malforus glanced around the room. "How about that kid over there?"

Timininious followed his gaze to the youth standing in line over at table two. The boy seemed to feel eyes upon him and turned to look at them. He paled and shook his head, backing up only to bump into the woman in line behind him. She glared at the boy and shoved him forward. He knocked into the half-orc in front of him who promptly turned around and punched him in the face. The boy dropped to his knees with a hand over his face, blood gushing from his nose.

"Impressive," remarked the third judge. "Is that a variation of the 'look that kills'?"

"Umm, yes." Timininious forced the evil grin he'd been practicing all afternoon since seeing the ad.

Maybe they would be happy with that and let him pass.

"Do the lightning." The woman rubbed her hands together. "I love lightning."

No such luck.

Gritting his teeth, Timininious closed his eyes, forming the words of the incantation in his mind. He concentrated on every syllable of the spell he knew by heart as he spoke the ancient tongue of magic.

Malforus gazed upward. "What the—"

Shouts filled the room, shattering the murmurs. Timininious's eyes flew open. *What the*, was right. He dropped his head into his hands and wished to disappear, but that would require another spell. He'd just have to make the best of this.

Blackberries rained down from the ceiling. They crushed underfoot, creating an ankle-deep slush of pulp. Winds blew through the room and thunder rumbled but not a lick of lightning appeared.

Malforus jumped up from his seat and ran over to shake Timininious. "Stop this at once!"

"I can't! It has to run its course," he shouted.

"This certainly isn't lightning."

Timininious took a deep breath and formulated an excuse. He'd always been good at those. "It's called Blackberry Storm. There must be some protection against lightning in the keep. Darkious Maximus Evil Overlord Extraordinaire and Master of the Nine Darknesses must be wise indeed to have such a spell of protection in place."

Shouts for the cleaning minions finally overtook the thunder and wind as the storm died down.

A thick woman with a booming voice entered the room. "Nobody move!" She stared them all down as if daring them to disobey.

Timinininous leaned close to Malforus. "Who is that?"

He whispered, "Satie. She's the current number two in charge and the leader of the supply minions."

The woman held the door open for a host of other uniformed minions to enter. They stepped carefully and carried armloads of buckets and bowls.

"Listen up everyone. We have an abundance of free food here. Bowls will be passed around and everyone is expected to fill them with blackberries." She signaled for the passing out of containers to begin. "I want these filled to the top, heaping. Anyone caught making a half-assed effort will be sent to the dungeons to be starved to death. Now, get to work."

While he waited for the buckets to come around, Timininious watched the imposing woman.

Something about her struck him odd. Then he figured out what it was. "Does she have a goatee?"

"Shh. She's a bit sensitive about that. You don't want to be on her bad side."

"Right. So, umm, since we're stuck here for a bit, I have to ask, am I evil enough?"

Malforus clapped him on the back. "You brought the tedium to a halt. For that alone, you have my vote." He turned to the other judges standing next to the table with blackberries halfway up to their knees. "What do you guys think?"

The woman raised an eyebrow. "Well, you made an entire room full of people, including those of us already employed, have to do menial labor. I'd call that true evil."

The man stood with his arms across his chest and a perturbed look on his face. "You've filled our food stores with fruit. Fruit, damn you. Evil people don't eat healthy food. Making them do so is plain evil. As much as I hate you for this, you're hired."

Timininious grinned but he remembered not to say thank you.

❧ 12 ❧

His Name is Darkious Maximus, Evil Overlord Extraordinaire and Master of the Nine Darknesses, And Don't You Forget It

"What is the meaning of this?" Ed pointed to the chaotic smattering of bones chained to the front of his precious keep.

Luc, his first in command during his absence, pointed to the line of men and creatures standing in the courtyard in a neat line. "First, let me say welcome back."

Bruce's brow furrowed and he cast a suspicious look at Ed. He said, "Excuse me, Ed, could you explain how you know this man? He looks evil."

The time for charades was over. Ed repeated his last used incantation in reverse. A feeling of rightness settled over him as his disguise dissolved. For the first time in three days, he reached up to stroke his goatee. It felt just how he remembered it, coarse and pointed. Darkious flicked the dust from his black shirt and shook out his black cloak. The silver embroidered DMs along the edges caught the light just as he liked, shimmering and exuding evil. He pulled the large, black onyx ring from his pocket and returned it to his finger.

"No," he said, "*this* is what evil looks like." Darkious struck his favorite pose, elbows thrust outward, his hands upon his hips, legs spread apart just so. He pivoted six degrees to get the maximum effect from the wind to toy with his cloak. And to finish off the look, he threw his head back and let out the deep evil laugh he saved for theatrical occasions such as this.

J'hal's mouth dropped open. "You? You're the evil overlord?"

"Indeed."

Bruce drew his sword. Mydeara drew her pan. The sheep let out a threatening *Baaa* in unison and the cattle snorted.

"Luc, keep these men under watch for a moment while I deal with the matter of the defacing of my keep."

Luc called for Satie, who after arriving moments

later, called for Malforus, who then called for a host of armed minions to surround the newcomers and their beasts.

"Now then, who is responsible for this mess?" Darkious eyed the minions Luc had been standing with when he'd come in.

Luc came to his side. "These are the publicity minions, oh Darkious Maximus, Evil Overlord Extraordinaire and Master of the Nine Darknesses. They are the ones who created this mess and used up all the prisoners in the dungeons in the process."

Empty dungeons? How could he prove his evilness without prisoners to torture? The answer clicked into his mind. "And who approved the prisoner requisition paperwork?"

Satie bowed her head and stepped forward. "I did, but in my defense, they didn't check the box that indicates that they planned on killing the prisoners. The plan they'd written stated they were going to nail the help wanted ads to them and parade them through the nearby villages."

An ogre stepped forward from the line. "That was my idea, but then that damned dwarf got it in this little bulbous head to spell everything out on the front of the keep."

"Excuses, excuses." It was just a matter of which one to kill first and how. Darkious looked the line over. Everyone stood above waist-high. "Where is this dwarf?"

Malforus stepped to his side. "I had that man properly punished yesterday—in keeping with paragraph twelve of the employee manual."

Darkious sneered. "The deluxe dungeon tour?"

His fourth in command bowed. "Yes, your evilness. We've also somewhat replenished the dungeons with discarded job applicants."

"Good work. At least someone was on top of things while I was out of the office." He glared at Satie and Luc. "Malforus, would you be so kind as to locate a member of our mobile torture team?"

"Right away, your evilness." The man dashed off and returned a moment later with an unfamiliar wizard wearing black robes embroidered with silver crescent moons and stars.

"You must be new?"

The man grinned behind his black goatee, his eyes beaming with enthusiasm. "Yes, your evilness. I'm Timininious."

"That's quite a name you have there. It doesn't sound very evil. I think we shall call you, Tim."

"Whatever you wish, your evilness."

"Well, Tim, I wish for you to punish a few people for us. Show me what you can do, that sort of thing. Would you prefer to torture them all at once or are you more of an individual sort of man?"

The wizard seemed to ponder that for a moment, pursing his lips and lowering his brow. "All at once would be a better show."

Darkious nodded and turned to the line of publicity minions. "Of course, you are all going to be punished." He held up his fingers and ticked one off. "Misfiling paperwork, defacing my keep, depleting my prisoners, and horrible judgment as to this project. I mean really, what is that even supposed to say?"

They all stared at the ground.

"And what ticks me off most is that these adventurers haven't even heard of me! Not a peep. That one"—he pointed to J'hal—"lives only a day away. What do I pay you people for?"

One of the minions turned to another. "I told you that nightmare machine wasn't working."

"You said you had it covered with those goblins you sent out to torment the countryside."

Another jumped in and another until the line became a mass of excuses and accusations. Darkious turned his back on them and addressed Satie. "You approved paperwork without following up. Join the others."

Her eyes grew wide and she shook her head. "But... but..."

"Luc, would you escort Satie to the lineup?"

"With pleasure, your evilness." Luc grabbed Satie's arm and tugged her over to the rest of the doomed minions.

"Oh, and Luc?"

"Yes?"

"You might as well stay right there too. I'm quite disappointed with how you managed things in my absence." Darkious basked in an evil grin. "Go on Tim, I think that's everyone for the moment. Give us a good show."

A flash of what looked like a serious case of performance anxiety flashed over the wizard's face. Darkious chuckled, basking in the unease his presence caused.

The wizard pulled himself up straight, cracked his knuckles, and eyed up the victims with a solemn stare. "As you wish, your evilness."

The sky grew dark with ominous clouds. Thunder rumbled. A cold wind whipped Darkious's cloak. He wasn't sure what the wizard intended with the stormy weather but it had a great effect on the line of doomed souls. They huddled together, muttering and watching the clouds with great dread.

Lightning struck the courtyard. It missed the line but did cause suitable screams and looks of terror. Darkious turned to see how his guests were enjoying the show. Within the confines of their guard-induced circle, the travelers appeared suitably awed, their eyes wide, their mouths agape. He spun back to the spectacle. The thunder faded away and the skies cleared.

Dense grey fog rose from the stones, masking any sign of the publicity minions. Then the wind picked up, dissipating the misty curtain. His minions had disappeared but, in their place, sat a clump of melon-sized white frogs. One croaked and blinked at him. "Riiibrains," it said as it hopped forward. The others sorted themselves out and joined their croaking with the first. A chorus of "Riiibrains" filled the courtyard.

Darkious cast a questioning glance at his new wizard. "What are those?"

Tim clasped his hands tightly together in front of him and bit down on his lower lip. He looked worried. "They are...umm...corpse frogs."

That sounded pretty evil, but he never trusted new help. "And just what is a corpse frog?"

"They come from the Swamp of Secrets out on the eastern plain." Tim's eyes lit up and his hands gestured grandly. "I've transformed your wayward minions into these undead creatures so that you may torture them in new and different ways. They will crave brains, preferably fresh and still warm, and will likely try just about anything to get them. You should be able to find many amusing ways to use this for entertainment."

"Most interesting." Darkious stroked his goatee. As with anything new, he couldn't wait to try it out. He perused the courtyard for victims. The travelers, he needed them for advertising—at least one or two of them, but he'd not chosen just yet. "You," he pointed to Malforus, "bring me a prisoner to play with."

Malforus snapped his fingers and pointed to one

of the nearby minions, who then ran off into the keep. They all stood around in the courtyard, no one speaking, with only the croaking of the corpse frogs to break the strained silence.

The minion returned ten minutes later, sweating and out of breath, with a scrawny grey-haired man in his grasp. He thrust the prisoner at Malforus and quickly stepped back, keeping an eye on the large pale frogs.

"Put him over there." Darkious pointed to the empty space between the onlookers and the corpse frogs.

Malforus did as he was told. The croaking rose to a frenzy. The corpse frogs sprang forward.

Two leapt away from the group to land on Bruce's head. Mydeara gasped, and held up her pan but seemed hesitant to strike. The frogs proceeded to thwack their long tongues at Bruce's eyeballs. He grabbed the corpse frogs and threw them against the keep. Two white bodies slid down the black stone, leaving a trail of luminescent ooze behind.

The knight leapt back, putting considerable space between him and the chaos at his feet. The man had collapsed onto the ground, waving his hands wildly over his head, trying to knock the frogs away. The corpse frogs beat at the stunned prisoner with their tongues. Within minutes, they had cracked his skull. They swarmed the brain nugget inside.

Darkious rubbed his hands together, enjoying

the fear and revulsion on this guest's faces. Even Malforus looked a bit pale. The wizard had done well with his punishment.

Bruce pointed to two white shapes limping toward them from the keep. "That throw didn't kill them?"

Tim shook his head. "Oh no. You can't kill a corpse frog so simply. The only way to kill them is to burn them."

"Fabulous." Darkious needed time to think. First, about how to best utilize these corpse frogs, and secondly about what to do with his visitors. "Tim, supervise the clean-up and containment of these creatures. I will play with them later. Malforus, please see that my guests are given rooms and their animals are cared for. Remind me to update your rank scroll tomorrow."

Malforus glanced at the visitors. "Rooms in the special wing?" He winked.

"Not just yet."

He looked disappointed. "As you wish, your evilness." Malforus strode over to the armed minions and belted out orders.

After being on the road for several days, Darkious missed his room. Everything was under control enough for the moment. It was time to retire.

He passed under the royal family arch, their heads preserved for all time so that they could all see him go about his business in what was once their castle. The black stone façade had done wonders for the transformation as had his good eye for interior decorating. Darkious paused to smile at the skull sconce beside the stairway. His favorite, the old captain of the guard—a man he had to admire for his capacity to withstand torture. The captain's skull smiled back at him as the candle behind his eyes danced.

Darkious took the stairs two at a time, anxious to be in his own bed. He rushed down the hall lined with doors to the rooms of his personal minions. His door stood at the end of the hall. He opened it and went inside.

Ah the smell of home, he thought as he breathed deep. In the fireplace sat the large chunk of brimstone he'd won by defeating the eighth darkness. Bats fluttered in the tall cage in the darkest corner of the room, their wings beating the iron bars.

"Welcome home, your evilness," said the scantily clad young woman chained to the bedpost.

"Hello, Agnes. Anything new while I was out?"

"Luc tried to fondle me again, your evilness."

"Luc is dead, or undead now I suppose." He shrugged. "Either way, he won't be bothering you again."

"The publicity minions have constructed a banner for your job fair."

"Yes, I've dealt with that too."

Agnes pouted. "I miss all the fun chained in here."

"You wanted the personal secretary position. Don't start griping about the working conditions now."

"Yes, but you were gone for days. Do you have any idea how lonely it is in here with just the bats and occasional messages delivered for you? I'd be of much better use chained to the outside of your door. You could cut the messenger minion that way."

"Now Agnes, why would I be looking to cut jobs when I'm trying to recruit more employees? This is why you are a secretary minion and not a corporate management minion."

Darkious unfastened his cloak and hung it on the hook on the wall. "As to being installed on the door, I know you'd like to see more of what is going on in the keep. I promise I'll let you out for a vacation real soon. We could spend a whole day together. Wouldn't that be nice?"

Her big blue eyes grew moist and she smiled. "I would love that. I'm sorry I complained."

Darkious waved off her apology and removed his shirt. He reached for the ties on his leggings. "Besides, how am I supposed to sleep with my secretary if she's out on the door?"

She blushed as he stepped out of his leggings. "You have a point."

⟡

Darkious's guests awaited him at the breakfast table. "I trust you all slept well?"

"It stinks in here," Bruce said.

"You'll get used to it. Evil has a scent. This is it."

The bard picked at his eggs. "These are barely cooked."

Darkious smiled. "I prefer my scrambled baby chicks be somewhat aware that they are being eaten."

Mydeara picked up the heel of bread on her plate. "And what is so evil about bread?"

"We pride ourselves in grinding the farmer with his wheat."

The girl set the bread down.

Darkious slurped a mouthful of eggs. "It's quite a process. If you grind the farmer outright, the flour turns red and it rots. Special care must be taken to kill the farmer, dry him thoroughly and *then* grind him. It took a few tries to work the process out, but I think it's well worthwhile." He took a bite of the bread. "Mmm, can't you just taste the evil?"

Of them all, J'hal seemed the least bothered by the meal, picking at it, but eating.

"Don't you want to know about the sausage?"

J'hal shrugged. "Let me guess, stuffed in human entrails?"

Had his secrets been leaked? Darkious scowled. "How did you know? Have you eaten here before?"

"Just seemed logical, I guess."

Evil wasn't logical. His guests needed a lesson.

Darkious waved an orc servant minion over. "My knife is not sharp."

The orc bowed low. "My humble apologies, your evilness."

Darkious stabbed him in the back and then pulled his knife free. "I guess it is sharp after all."

The orc fell to the floor. The others stood stock straight in their seats, but J'hal merely glanced over and chewed his bread. Did nothing faze this man? Darkious found himself greatly annoyed.

'arold cleared his throat, "We get that you are evil. There's no need to kill anyone."

"It's breakfast, for goodness' sake. Someone always dies before breakfast is over. How else am I supposed to get motivated for the day ahead?"

'arold's voice quaked. "Go for a walk? Write in a journal? Maybe take up painting sunrises?"

Darkious glared at the little man and picked up a tart from the platter in front of him. He bit into it and then spit it out all over his plate. "Fruit? What is the meaning of this? This is not on my list of approved foods. Bring me the cook!"

An old woman lumbered in, her girth barely fitting through the archway. She took one look at the pastry in his hand and rolled her eyes. "Oh, them."

"Tell me there is a hint of the woman who picked these in the tart?"

"Your evilness, they are *black*berries. What is more evil than black?"

This was true. His anger drained a bit. Then he remembered what 'arold had said bout the color. He glared at the bard again before turning back to the cook. "Where did we get them? I don't recall claiming any lands bearing blackberries."

"The new torture minion, some wizardly sort, he conjured them up."

"Tim?"

"Sounds right."

"Was it some sort of evil magic that conjured them?"

The cook scratched her chin rolls. "It was part of his evil audition." Her eyes lit up. "Countless souls stood in these berries before being sentenced to the dungeons."

"Well that's something, I guess." Darkious picked up the tart and tried another bite. "They are quite good."

"Yes, your evilness." The cook hurried from the room.

Darkious addressed his guests, "Now then, who would like a tour?"

Bruce said, "You're giving us a tour? Aren't you supposed to lock us in the dungeon or something?"

"Why would I do that?"

"Because you're evil?"

Darkious laughed. "There will be plenty of time for that sort of thing later." After I pick a couple of you to spread the word, he thought. The bard seemed like the best choice, but he worried that the horrible little song monger would paint him in an unflattering light. The girl was his next choice but would people write off her recounting of the terrors she'd witnessed as common womanly hysterics? That left J'hal or Bruce. If he let the obvious hero go, then what sort of challenge did he pose as an evil overlord? The knight needed to die, that much was certain, and preferably in some great battle of wills that highlighted his evilness. J'hal puzzled him. This blithe young man was the one who was slated to overthrow him? The rightful king? Someone had gone through some trouble to hide the boy away. There had to be some great secret, some magic, some special bloodline that made this one man stand out. *The son*, the seer had called him.

"So J'hal, your parents, did they ever mention this castle?"

"Nope." He took a second heel of bread from the platter in the middle of the table.

"Did they ever tell you stories of a great destiny in store for you?" Darkious asked.

"Nope."

"Have you ever had any dreams that seemed to guide your way, reveal secrets, or imply a god or goddess favored you?"

J'hal arched an eyebrow. "You sure ask a lot of questions."

Darkious sneered. "I'm choosing which of you to

kill first. Answer me."

He shrugged. "Nope. I don't dream much. My parents were apparently not my parents. They never mentioned this castle or any other royal family. Until yesterday, I was content to be a farmer for the rest of my life. I've never even considered any 'great destiny'."

"Very good. That settles it."

Bruce scowled. "Settles what?"

Darkious pushed his chair back and stood. "Let's go for a walk, shall we?"

"No really, settled what? If you're going to kill one of us, I'd like to know who," said Bruce.

"That would take the evil out of it, wouldn't it?"

'arold nodded. "'e 'as a point."

Darkious grinned, thinking of Agnes the night before. "I'm rather fond of points. Let's go see some." He rubbed his hands together and led the way from the dining hall to the stairway leading to the dungeon.

At the sign engraved 'Evil Dungeon ahead, watch your step', he paused to make sure everyone read it. Lawsuits were wicked things, and while he was fond of wicked, lawyers made him cringe. Most of them had been killed within his first weeks of taking over the country, but they still seemed to pop up on occasion. No need to take chances.

He pointed to the railing. "Use it. It's there for a reason." Boots scraped across the stone steps behind him as they all tromped down the twisting stairway.

At the bottom, they stopped at the dungeon master's desk.

"Greetings, your evilness. To what do we owe this special visit?" The troll behind the desk offered him a nervous snaggle-toothed smile.

"Taking a tour with some guests." Darkious indicated the four bodies behind him.

"I see, your evilness. Will this be the standard or the deluxe tour?" he asked with a wink.

"Just the guided one for the time being."

The dungeon master looked disappointed. "The last round of applicants helped to replenish our stock as did the batch of folks with delinquent tax debt that was delivered yesterday. You should find everything well supplied, your evilness. Please let me know if you need anything during your visit."

Darkious gestured for his guests to follow him. "Come on then, I'd like to show you some new weaponry we're working on."

J'hal looked around, relief clear on his face. "My parents are here then? Not up in that mess on the front wall?"

"Probably, yes. We'll see about finding them in a bit." Darkious rubbed his hands together. Maybe he could find them and confine the reunion to the inside of the cell. Yes, that plan had a nice evil ring to it. With a jaunty step, he headed into the dungeon, toward the sound of clanging metal and a roaring furnace.

"You keep your blacksmith in the dungeon?" asked J'hal.

"What better place to test new weapons?" He led them to the alcove where a giant troll blacksmith pounded out a strip of iron."

"Is this some sort of magic weapon?" Bruce asked.

"No, but never underestimate a weapon forged in evil," said Darkious.

'arold held up a finger. "I believe a weapon must be forged in fire. Can fire be evil? I don't think so. Fire is not living, so it cannot 'ave intent. But the one who lights the fire could 'ave evil intent." He looked the blacksmith over. "Forged *by* evil. Yes, that would be the correct way to say it."

Darkious snarled at the annoying bard. "Are you correcting me?"

'arold stepped back, losing himself behind Mydeara and J'hal.

"Let's go on then, shall we?" Darkious led them past the rack where the leftovers from its last victim were being cleared away.

They stopped at the endless hall of cells. It wasn't really endless, that was a trick of neatly placed mirrors. Passing by, his guests didn't seem to notice that it was an illusion as their gasps were suitably audible.

"Watch your step here." Darkious stayed on the far edge of the safety railing surrounding the burbling lava pit.

'arold examined the lava. "'ow do you keep this contained? Why doesn't it burn through the rock floor and swallow the castle?"

"I paid an earth wizard to convert the hot springs into a lava pit. He did a harnessing spell to prevent it from getting out of control."

J'hal approached the railing but wisely did not touch it. "What do you need lava for? Why not just use fire?"

"Lava is more exotic, don't you think?"

J'hal shrugged. "I suppose."

Frustrated with the apathetic young man, Darkious paused the tour. "Fine, you want to see how we utilize the lava?" Darkious waved to a passing minion. "Bring me something to play with."

"Yes, your evilness." The man hobbled off and returned with a hunched elderly woman.

Bruce stammered, "What's she done to deserve being imprisoned? You can't just go around locking up little old women."

"I can," said Darkious. "I'm evil. Besides, she's a member of some sisterhood. Women organizing themselves..." He shook his head. "Now, that's trouble waiting to happen. I'm doing the countryside a favor by keeping all the members of this crazy coven locked up."

"But you're not locking them up." Bruce glared at him. "You're killing them."

Despite being in one of his favorite places,

Darkious found his frustration growing. "I wasn't even around for the whole banner fiasco. That matter has been suitably resolved. Let it go."

"I can't let it go. I'm a knight. We're supposed to protect people against evil overlords like you."

His calm returned. This was the kind of stuff he was looking for, a zealous knight goaded into duty. Oh, the fun he would have with this one. "I like to think I'm not like the others." Darkious grabbed the old woman and lashed her hands to the bar hanging beside the pit of lava.

She struggled against her bonds, shrieking and cursing all of them. Then she caught sight of Bruce.

"Save me! You must save me!"

Bruce drew his sword. "I'm trying to. Quit your yelling."

"I know about the son! The son must be protected!"

"Lady, what are you raving about?" asked Bruce.

"The son must never meet the father! Remember this, knight. Remember this and be charged now to prevent it from happening."

Bruce cocked his head and furrowed his brow. "What are you on about? I have no idea what son or father you mean. Besides, I'm already on a quest, and I've lost track of how many side quests. I'm not looking to take on any more work, and a charity case to boot."

"But this is important!" the woman yelled.

Her blathering hurt Darkious's ears. He cranked

the winch handle. The woman rose into the air. He shifted the lever beside him. The woman swung out over the sizzling pit.

She shrieked. "No! Hear me, knight, you must protect the son."

Bruce turned to Darkious. "As much as I loathe your evilness, I'm with you on destroying this sisterhood. Are they all this demanding?"

Darkious cranked the winch a couple more notches, lowering the screaming woman. "Some of them are worse. Spouting cryptic prophesies, threatening to curse my loins, foretelling my doom." He rolled his eyes. "Tiring, I tell you. Endless blathering. Once a woman gets past her childbearing years, I swear they live on with the sole purpose to natter the rest of us to death."

J'hal put his hands over his ears "Speed it up already."

Mydeara turned away. 'arold walked off a distance.

Bruce yelled back at the old woman. "Shut up!"

"You call yourself a knight?" She spat at him.

"Hey lady, I told you, I'm on a quest already. I can't go wandering about accepting an endless number of side quests and never giving my all to any of them, now can I? Besides, you're not even telling me what the quest is, you're just nattering like my crazy grandma did when I was a boy—spinning silly stories about boys with great destinies and mysterious parentage."

Her eyes lit up. "Yes! That's exactly what I'm saying!"

"Oh, please." J'hal, Bruce, and Darkious said in unison. They all looked at each other and cracked a smile.

Bruce sighed and lifted his sword again. "All right, Darkious Maximus, I can't—"

Darkious scowled. "You are in my keep, touring my dungeons, witnessing the torture of my prisoners, you will show respect and use my full name."

"Right. Sorry. Darkious Maximus, Evil Overlord Extraordinaire and Master of the Nine Darknesses, as much as I am sick of this woman's ramblings, I cannot let you actually dip her in lava."

"I didn't plan on dipping her."

"Oh good." Bruce lowered his sword. "So, this is more of a mind game sort of thing?"

"No. I mean to submerge her until the flesh melts off her bones."

"Oh." Bruce glanced at the old woman and brought his sword back up. "Then I'm afraid I'm going to have to ask you to step away from the winch."

Darkious gave it another click. "I could do that." Another click. "But I'd just have a minion take over for me. Would you find that more acceptable?"

"No."

Darkious shrugged. "I had a feeling that would be your answer." Another click.

Bruce stepped toward him.

"Gather 'round my minions and witness the glory of your overlord!" Darkious swirled his cloak over his shoulders and drew his own sword.

"When did you start wearing a sword?" Bruce crept closer; his sword held at the ready.

"I always wear a sword."

'arold piped up, "Actually, your evilness, if I may, you wear a scabbard. You carry a sword."

They both turned to glare at the bard.

Bruce nodded toward 'arold. "How about we trade 'arold for the old woman? You can do whatever you like to him."

'arold surged forward. "Now wait a minute!"

As much as Darkious wanted to silence the annoying bard, the woman was already in place and he rather had his mind set on killing her. He hated changing his plans at the last minute. "We can kill 'arold later. Maybe I'll feed him to the corpse frogs. What do you think about that 'arold? Hmm? A brain as big as yours ought to keep them sated for a day or two."

The bard halted his forward charge. "My brain isn't all that big."

"No? Well then, maybe you should shut your mouth more often," said Mydeara.

'arold slunk back into the shadows. J'hal and Mydeara's attention was nicely glued to the show about to start.

Bruce's sword hit Darkious's, sending an unpleasant vibration down his arm. It had been a long time since he'd fought anyone with a sword. Not since he'd defeated the previous master of the first darkness. Darkious took a swing at the knight. Perhaps calling upon his darknesses would add some terror to the situation. You just can't pack in enough terror, he said to himself.

While his body went through the motions, doing his best not to look like an utter lout in combat with a trained knight barricaded behind plate armor while he wore nothing but his clothes and a cloak, Darkious began to chant.

"Quit that." Bruce knocked Darkious's sword aside, almost landing a hit on his side.

Darkious danced back, mindful of the railing and the lava. A suction formed beside him, growing and spreading. Dirt rose from the floor, flowing into the vortex. Darkious scowled. He'd have to talk with the cleaning minions about that.

J'hal looked the vortex over with interest. "What is that?"

"This is the first level of darkness. A portal into the black nothingness. Bruce, would you like to take a closer look?"

"No, thanks. It's very nice though."

"I'm afraid, I must insist." Darkious resumed his chant. The vortex detached itself from his side and drifted forward.

Bruce stepped back, keeping an even pace with the oncoming black maw. They matched each other step for step, Bruce's retreat, and the vortex's approach.

"Keep moving." The elderly woman yelled.

"I am. Are you blind?"

"It's really hot over this pit, would you mind getting me out of here?"

"I'm kind of busy."

The woman mocked, "I'm kind of busy." She stuck out her tongue. "I'm kind of dying from the heat! Get moving, you so-called knight!"

Gathering that Bruce would be heading for the winch, Darkious considered the other darknesses at his disposal and then settled on his choice. He rubbed the ring on his finger while whispering the words of release. A ten-foot-tall golem appeared next to him as if stepping from thin air into the dungeon. Even his gathered minions gasped. Darkious grinned, his blood pumping and his body singing with energy.

"Behold, the third darkness!" Darkious handed his sword to the golem. "Kill that man, my pet."

The golem, hunched under the low ceilings in the dungeon, took the sword from Darkious and trundled toward Bruce. He let out a low rumbling, "Gaaah," and swung the sword in wide arcs.

Darkious checked his audience. The minions pointed at Bruce and jeered, laughing and making bets as to his method of demise. J'hal seemed excited for the first time since he'd entered the keep, cheering both for and against Bruce and appearing most enthusiastic when swords collided, no matter which side came out ahead.

Bruce managed to get one crank of the winch before his hair started to fly sideways as the vortex drew closer. The Golem's sword reached him seconds later, clanking against the knight's armor and sending Bruce stumbling sideways. He slammed against the railing. A loud clang echoed in the vast chamber.

There had to be something else Darkious could do. One more thing to really sell the moment. He stroked his goatee. A sneer broke out upon his lips along with another chant.

Bruce recovered, tumbling forward and slicing at the golem's legs. Before the golem could make use of his longer reach, Bruce rolled out of range yet again.

"Gaaah," said the golem.

A grey cloud appeared over Darkious's head, swirling and churning, buzzing like a mass of black flies. He pointed to Bruce. The cloud shot over the lava pit after the knight. As it neared the other side, the cloud sizzled and shook. It picked up speed and zoomed right past Bruce, hitting the dungeon wall and bouncing off again. The cloud burbled and swelled, growing blacker with each second.

J'hal sidled up to Darkious. "What is that crazy thing?"

"The sixth darkness."

"Interesting." J'hal rubbed his chin.

The sixth darkness slammed into Bruce, knocking him back but bouncing off the plate armor. The Golem's sword sliced through the repelled cloud, causing the cloud to hiss and separate. The two halves came together and hissed even louder, pursuing the third darkness. The golem dropped its sword to wave its hands around its head to try to stave off the angry cloud. It screamed, "Gaaaah!"

The sixth darkness swarmed around the head of the third. The first darkness, the portal, finally caught up to the golem's side. Bruce dashed by them all, grabbing the golem's sword and retreating.

Something hit Darkious in the back of the head. Something flat and metal, it clanged against his skull a second time. He spun around. Mydeara held her pan up for a third strike.

"You leave Bruce be! Call them off!"

"The darknesses are hungry. They always are. They will not rest until they are fed. Unless you are offering yourself up in his stead?"

The girl's resolve faltered.

Darkious couldn't help but rub it in. "See, this is why you're not a hero. Heroes are supposed to offer themselves up for those they care about."

"I never said I was a hero." Mydeara swung her pan again, this time hitting Darkious smack in the face.

"Oww!" Darkious was about to demand help but then he remembered he was supposed to be putting on the grand show to impress...well, someone. Once the knight was dead, he'd figure out the next step. He kicked the girl to the ground and then spun around to check on his darknesses.

The cloud around the golem's head grew larger yet. Its enraged screams filled the air, echoing off the stone walls. Bruce charged, plunging his sword into the golem's gut. It screamed even louder and fell backward, tumbling into the portal and taking the buzzing cloud into the darkness with it.

Silence filled the dungeon.

Darkious broke it. "Noooooooooooooooooo!"

J'hal shook his head. "Evil feeds on evil. Interesting."

"Must you keep saying that?" Darkious said, his voice so high it verged on cracking.

"Sorry." J'hal left his side and went to check on Bruce.

Darkious watched the young man walk, confident and striding. Then it struck him. J'hal's movements reminded him of all the times he'd practiced walking in front of the mirror in his room.

He stroked his goatee. The shape of J'hal's face caught his attention. The jawline, the chin, they were so familiar. He imagined J'hal with a goatee. His breath caught in his throat. He needed to sit down.

One of his minions came to his side. "Is everything

all right, your evilness?"

"Go out into the stables for me. Count the livestock that this lot brought with them."

"At once, your evilness." The minion bowed and scampered off.

The old woman yelled, "Hello? I'm still up here!"

Bruce glanced at Darkious.

Darkious sighed. "Fine." He waved a minion to the winch. There were bigger things at stake here. Besides, he could always dunk the old woman in the lava after the tour was over.

But the heir? How could this happen? "J'hal, come here a moment."

The young man left the knight's side. "What is it? You look pale. More than usual. Is there something wrong?"

Other than the fact that three of his darknesses had just been defeated? He exhaled and inhaled, gathering his wits.

"If you could stay right here for a moment. I'm waiting for some news that may pertain to you." And for his heart to stop pounding. Darkious put his hand to his chest and took several deep breaths. His mind spun, revisiting faded memories from eighteen years ago. The girl in the orchard? He didn't see anything of her face in J'hal. The woman who brought him meals when he was too busy pouring over his evil tomes to remember to eat? Perhaps the sisters who had served in his minions during his early days. He remembered the twins fondly. J'hal didn't strike him as the evil type. Then again, he'd been raised out of the whole evil loop. Maybe it was all an act. Maybe he was truly evil under that bland farm boy exterior. Maybe he had some secret weapon and was just waiting for the opportune time to use it. Darkious resisted the urge to bite his nails, distracting himself with pondering other motherly options.

This was the son who was supposed to overthrow him? He might be handsome and well-built, which was little surprise given where he'd come from, but cunning and devious he was not. Seventeen years was a long time for a prophecy to go awry.

"Your evilness," the minion sidled up to his other side. "There are thirteen sheep and fourteen cows."

Darkious nodded and shooed the minion away. Twenty-seven animals, four men, that still left them two short. Relief shot through him. J'hal might have been in the right place at the right time, but he didn't have the numbers.

The boy would have to work hard to raise thirty-three men to fight Darkious if he were surrounded by minions for the rest of his life. He couldn't really consider killing his son now that he knew the truth. Not unless it was for something monumental. There had to be some way to put the boy to optimal use. But first, the truth needed to come to light so he could separate him from this motley lot.

"J'hal, I have something I need to tell you,

something important."

"Hurry, do something," said the old woman now standing next to Bruce, rubbing her reddened wrists.

"You didn't even thank me for freeing you yet." Bruce shook his head. "And you think you can still nag me?"

J'hal peered into the hall of cells behind them. "Where are my parents?" he asked. "Are they down here somewhere? My mother? My father?"

"Run, find them! Don't listen to this evil man!" shouted the old woman. She made shooing motions with her hands.

"Shouldn't you be escaping while he's distracted or something?" J'hal suggested to the old woman.

"Pay attention dammit. This is a monumental moment," said Darkious

J'hal turned to face him. "Fine. What is it?"

"No!" the old woman hurled herself at Darkious, hands curled into claws.

Darkious summoned the second darkness, unleashing a bolt of black lightning. The woman shrieked as the bolt pierced her stomach and then she vanished as the bolt transported her back into the realm where darkness dwelt.

They all stared at the spot where the woman had been, a suitable level of awe on their faces. Darkious seized the moment to make his announcement.

"J'hal, *I* am your father."

"What?" He laughed. Not only laughed but threw

his head back and really laughed.

The sound warmed Darkious's heart. It was his own laugh, coming out of this new, younger body. New and younger. He pursed his lips as a devious thought came to mind. If he took good care of the boy, when the time came for his own body to fail, he could transfer himself into the younger one. Oh, what a plan! He rubbed his hands together and grinned.

J'hal paused in his laughing. "What are you doing that for?"

"Umm, nothing. Never mind. Where were we? Oh yes, I am your father."

"You're serious?"

"Very. I've concluded that you are the spawn of my first secretary."

"How could you not know?"

"Well, she worked for me for several months, but then I had to fire her for taking sloppy dictation. It would be just like her to set you against me with this whole concocted 'you're the rightful king' set up. Vindictive witch."

His face fell. "So I'm not really royalty?"

"Not exactly. But I do rule the country, and you are my son, so I suppose if you want to call that royalty then you could. Evil Overlords are part of the ruling class after all."

"I'd rather gotten attached to the idea of having King in my name."

"I'll tell you what, you come up with whatever name you like. You should get rid of the elvish name anyway. It's misleading."

J'hal tapped his chin with his finger and sunk into a deep thought pose. "How about, J'hal, King of Gambreland?"

Darkious frowned. The boy lacked imagination, that much was clear. "How about something more original? Something like: the spawn of evil incarnate, his highness John, the most dark one."

The young man's eyes lit up. "Oh, I like that! Are you sure that it's not too much?"

"Too much? You're my son, who cares if it's too much. You can do whatever you want."

"I can?"

"Sure."

J'hal jumped up and down. "Did you hear that guys? This is my father! I've found my real father!"

❧ 13 ❧

The Spawn of Evil Incarnate, His Highness John, the Most Dark One Earns His Name

Bruce scowled. "I hate to tell you this, J'hal, but your father is the Evil Overlord we came here to overthrow. The one with your parents in this very dungeon."

J'hal pouted. "Maybe I don't want to overthrow him. I mean, if I'm his son, I'll inherit the kingdom after he dies. There's no need to overthrow anyone."

"How do you plan to free the people from the reign of terror set upon them by this Evil Overlord?"

The overlord cleared his throat.

"Sorry," said Bruce, "Darkious Maximus, Evil Overlord Extraordinaire, Master of the Nine Darknesses. You came here to save your people from him."

"I don't appreciate this kind of talk." His father pointed to Mydeara and 'arold. "Minions, put those two in a cell."

Three minions charged the girl and the bard. Mydeara raised her pan. Harold put his harp behind his back and cowered behind Mydeara.

J'hal raised his hand and glowered at his father. "Stop! Don't touch them."

The minions hesitated just the slightest bit. J'hal quite liked this new situation. He had a new father, an important one, and now minions were listening to him. Sort of. This beat plowing fields and milking cows any day.

Here, he had power. A new thrilling energy sizzled through him.

"You said I could do whatever I wanted," said J'hal. "I want those two kept unharmed."

"Fine," his father said through clenched teeth. He redirected his minions. "Kill the knight then."

"No!" J'hal stepped in front of Bruce. "What's gotten into you?" He gave his father an accusing glare. "One minute you're giving us the guided tour and the next you're out to have us killed."

"Not you. Just them."

"Why? What harm have they brought to you?"

"None, yet. I plan to keep it that way."

"How about we let them go," J'hal suggested. "We could make them promise not to harm you. And while we're at it, Father, I want my parents freed and sent safely home with their cows as well as the chickens the tax collectors took."

His father grimaced and then exhaled loudly. "Fine." He motioned for one of the nearby minions to fulfill his son's requests.

"What is it with you and killing anyway?" J'hal asked.

"I'm evil. It's what I do." He said proudly, clapping J'hal on the shoulder. "And so are you. Now, I believe it's time to make an announcement. Attention everyone!"

Once the nearby minions had gathered around, the overlord held out his hand to J'hal. "I'd like to introduce my son, The Spawn of Evil Incarnate, His Highness John, the Most Dark One."

The host of minions clapped and bowed. Tears welled in Mydeara's eyes and 'arold stood with his mouth hanging open.

Bruce shook his head and sighed. "I don't suppose you'd let us get away with addressing you as The Spawn? Maybe just John? I can barely get your father's name out, for goodness' sake, and now you're throwing that monster of a name at me?"

"For you, Bruce, I'll accept it. The same goes for you Mydeara and 'arold."

"Uhh, thanks." Mydeara smiled weakly.

John. He'd have to get used to his new name. He glanced around, he was going to have to get used to a lot of things, but the sizzling in his veins assured him he could do just about anything. For the first time in his life, he could think clearly. It was as if a fog on his mind had been lifted.

"Your evilness!" A minion came running down the stairs. "There's been an incident in the barn. It was horrible, your evilness." He shook his head. "Terrible. Blood everywhere."

That didn't sound like something he wanted to get used to. John glanced at his father.

"Terrible, you say? I suppose we should take a look then," his father said, leading them toward the stairs.

When they reached the top, they all hurried outside. The barn doors stood open, though the view was blocked by a crowd of milling minions.

His father shoved them aside, barreling through. John followed in his wake.

A towering troll minion stood his ground. "You really don't want to go in there, your evilness."

"Maybe I do. And who are you to question me?"

"I was promoted to head visual protection minion last month, your evilness. I saw the whole thing, perhaps you would like me to relay what happened?"

"I'd like to see it myself and then you can relay." The overlord shouldered his way through the remaining wall of gawking minions.

John used his broad shoulders to do the same, coming to stand beside his father inside the barn.

The sight before him was truly worthy of being called horrific and terrible. A male minion stood in the middle of the barn with a serene look upon his face. A glow emanated from his body as though a candle burned within him. In place of his eyes sat two pools of luminescence. His uniform, no longer black, shone a brilliant white and the silver DM on his chest had vanished. At his feet lay the remains of his goatee, leaving his face clean-shaven.

"You," said a voice that sent a tremor through the barn and the minions cower. The white man raised his hand in slow motion and pointed at John.

John's heart stuttered and his mouth went dry. Then he realized the glowing minion was pointing at his father, not him.

"I'm told you have attacked my chosen's chosen."

The overlord scowled and took a step forward. "I don't know who you are, but I'm going to ask nicely just one time for you to get out of my barn."

"You don't know me?"

No one piped up with any helpful information. John glanced at his father, who appeared to be thinking hard.

John glanced around the barn for clues. The roof seemed intact, so no crashing to the ground from the skies. The walls appeared sound, and no strange beasts stood stomping or snorting nearby, so he did not arrive through any amazing means. Other than a bit of scorched dirt around the feet of the man in white and the sheep practically bowing before him, there was no sign of anything untoward. For some mystical or magical creature, he seemed quite understated. It was little wonder that he was unheard of. His father made much more of an impression, John thought proudly.

"Sorry, no. I'm coming up with nothing," said the overlord.

One of the sheep shot a glare at John. Those creatures were not like other sheep. Something was very strange about them and the way they followed Bruce around.

The glowing minion spoke. "Behold, I am Hucker, God of sheep. My blessed sheep have taken this knight as their chosen one. You have seen fit to fight him, so will you also fight me?"

Fighting a god seemed like a bad idea, even for an evil overlord.

"I've got better things to do than fight sheep gods in barns, but let me see if my schedule has any openings." His father snapped his fingers.

A minion stepped forth with a scroll in hand. "Your evilness, I'm afraid we have a rather tight schedule today. The breakfast with the newcomers and the dungeon tour has already bumped some of your planned daily activities into tomorrow."

John pondered this for a few moments as he gazed at the god. "So what are we going to do about him?"

"Well, we can't kill him. Not that I don't want to, but killing gods," his father leaned in close and whispered, "is a smidge out of my league."

John winked. "I see." He cleared his throat. "If we let Bruce and the sheep go, perhaps the god will leave us alone."

The overlord pursed his lips. "Perhaps, and we are in a bit of a bind. I'll consider it."

Pleased he'd thought of something useful, John listened closely for his next chance to prove himself.

His father stepped forward. "I bask in your presence and all that," he twirled his finger. "If I let all your chosen go, will you leave? You're sucking the evil out of my castle with every second that you're around."

The god glanced at the sheep. "You won't kill Bruce or the one called Mydeara?"

"No."

John noticed that Hucker hadn't mentioned 'arold. "What about the bard?"

"The sheep say the bard has no rhythm and silencing him would be a favor to everyone," said Hucker.

"I can kill 'arold then?" asked the overlord

"I'm afraid not. See, I'm a god, and we must cherish all life. Besides, how bad can he be?"

John reached back and grabbed the bard from two rows behind him, hauling 'arold forward. He thrust the bard at the god. "Sing him a song."

'arold stammered something about needing to tune his harp after the dampness of the dungeons.

"Get to it then. You're keeping a god waiting, after all," said John.

'arold nodded and got busy tuning his strings.

Not that it would help, John knew. He shared a disgusted look with his father. The bard was sure to be struck down by the second line.

The bard cleared his throat and plucked a few strings. "I've never played for a god before."

Hucker looked impatient. The sheep and the cattle looked ready to stampede.

Sheep be wonderful fluffy creatures
Their 'ooves, and wool and other great features
Do 'omage to their god in many ways
By our brave knight's side they stays
Through long cold nights
And many frights
We praise the friend of the earth mother, 'ucker

The god's mouth dropped open. "What did you just call me?"

Harold stepped back. "'ucker?"

"Do you wish to die?"

"Of course not, your most 'oly 'ucker."

"I've had enough of you." Hucker raised his arm, extending his finger toward 'arold. "I won't kill you, but I can't stand another moment of your presence. Be gone."

A shot of lightning snaked out from his finger and hit Harold in the chest. The bard spasmed, his back arching as his body floated upward toward the rafters of the barn. A bright light built up around him, swirling and spinning, turning 'arold in slow circles. He turned faster and faster, a warm wind picking up and tugging at the hair of all who looked on. And then, in a sudden flash of light, 'arold ceased to be. In his place was nothing but air and rafters.

John scowled. "I thought you said you couldn't kill him?"

"He's not dead. I merely sent him to an alternate reality, a world much like this one but without any of us in it to be plagued by his horrible songs."

The overlord grinned. "Well then, we're all in agreement. You'll leave. Bruce goes free. I get to keep my kingdom and my son helps me rule instead of overthrowing me like that stupid prophecy said. Everyone is happy."

John gasped. "There was a prophecy?"

"There was, but now that I've met you..." His father shrugged. "I'm sure your mother made all that stuff up just to screw with me."

"Yes, that sounds about right." John smiled blandly as he took stock of his father and the surrounding minions with calculating eyes. Inside, his thoughts were spinning. He stroked his bare chin.

Perhaps it was time he grew a goatee.

His father had turned his attention back to the god. "Can we call it good now?"

Hucker glanced at the sheep and nodded. "Yes, I think we are. See that no harm comes to those under my protection, and you will not see me again."

"Sounds good. Now, get out of my barn."

Hucker narrowed his eyes, focusing the beam of light shining within so that it reflected upon the overlord's chest.

"I mean to say, it was nice of you to stop by, but I really must get back to work now."

John made a note to steer clear of gods no matter what his future held.

"That's better," said Hucker. "Enjoy ruling with your son. Oh, and Bruce? You've got a surprise waiting for you near the Sea of Sickness to thank you for your service to *my* chosen one. Enjoy." Hucker nodded and then closed his eyes, shutting off the light within the body he inhabited. The body fell to the ground, an empty husk. Nothing more than skin without bones to give it shape. A puddle of man.

John shuddered. For a good god, Husker still managed an impressive evil impression. He was going to have to work on that too.

"Father, do you mind if I get some practice in here?"

"Practice doing what?"

"Being evil."

"Oh, of course." The overlord smiled proudly.

John spun around. "Bruce, take Mydeara and your sheep and get out. You've outstayed your welcome here."

Bruce's brows drew together. "Welcome? When have we been welcome here? We came here intent to overthrow the evil overlord—"

The overlord cleared his throat.

"That guy," Bruce pointed to Darkious, "Darkious Maximus, Evil Overlord Extraordinaire and Master of the Nine Darknesses. But rather than overthrow evil, you've seen fit to join it." He uttered a frustrated growl. "You have no idea how bad this makes me look. It's embarrassing. Are you sure you wouldn't like me to run my sword through his heart?"

John laughed. "That really won't be necessary, but I do admire your knightly self and Mydeara's plucky nature, so be gone with you. I must take my place at my father's side."

Mydeara shook her head. "Are you really comfortable going by The Spawn of Evil Incarnate, His Highness John, the Most Dark One?"

John nodded. "I rather like it. It has a good ring to it, don't you think?"

"A death knell, more like," Mydeara muttered and then turned away. "Come on Bruce, we best get out of here before anyone changes their mind."

"I don't suppose I could get the dagger back that I lent you?" asked Bruce.

John removed the dagger from his belt. He considered throwing it at Bruce to prove his evilness to his father, but then caught sight of the skin husk Hucker had left behind. "I suppose so. But I'm not sharpening it or cleaning it." He stabbed at one of the thick barn beams a few times, doing his best to dull the blade before tossing it at Bruce's feet.

Bruce grabbed the dagger like it was some poor wounded creature. "Could we get paid? Perhaps just a little? After all, we did find your parents. Alive, I might add. We could escort them home if you like."

"For a small fee," added Mydeara.

John looked to his father, hoping for a little advice on how to evilly handle this situation.

"Tim? Where's my new wizard?" called his father.

Minions parted to let an older man through. "Yes, your evilness? How might I serve you?"

"You know what?" said Bruce, "we'll just be going then. No charge. I need to fill my quota of charity cases anyway."

The knight backed away and beckoned to the sheep. The wooly creatures followed. Mydeara stuck to his side.

"Hey Bruce," John called out before they could get out of the barn. "The Wall is due north of here. When you leave the capital, just keep going right out of the gate. You should be there in a few days."

"Thank you." Bruce waved. "Hey, I hope it works out for you here."

"Thanks. Good luck on your quest." John waved back, smiling all the while.

"What was that all about?" His father asked as they walked back to the keep. "I thought you were going to practice being evil."

"I was. The wall is more northwest and will take them months to reach by foot. Straight north is the Desert of Despair. They'll likely starve before then unless Bruce crosses Hucker and eats one of his sheep."

His father slapped him on the back. "Well son, I have to say, I'm impressed."

John grinned, taking in the keep that would be his. Perhaps, someday, very soon.

❦ 14 ❦

Bruce And The Damsel

Bruce trudged onward through the endless sand. A few days, he scoffed. Yeah right. It seemed the evil overlord's son was more evil than Bruce had given him credit for. They were lost and in the middle of nothing with the last of their food eaten over a month ago. Since then they'd been foraging on the occasional scraggly berry bush, bugs, and a few unlucky snakes. The sheep gave him warning glances every time his stomach rumbled. Mydeara slogged along beside him.

Afternoon drew into evening and he was about ready to call a halt for the night when he caught the sound of voices on the wind. "Did you hear that?"

Mydeara lifted her head. "No. Wait, yes. People! Maybe they'll have food and water."

They dashed over the hills of sand to come to a

rise that afforded a view of the valley below. Fifty men and women danced around a raging fire that reflected in the pond behind their encampment. The women sang and danced while the men beat drums and cheered them on.

"Who are these people?" Mydeara whispered.

"I'm not sure, but I smell food. Let's go find out."

The smell of fresh roasting pork wafted at them as they drew closer. Saliva pooled in Bruce's mouth.

"Help!" An urgent call, just loud enough to hear over the singing, caught his attention.

Bruce said, "Someone is in trouble."

Mydeara nodded. "No kidding. They teach you that great reasoning in knight school?"

"We covered it on the first day, thank you very much."

They crept down the hill, hoping the people around the fire were too distracted to notice them.

"Help! I'm over here," said a female voice

"Could you yell a little quieter? You're going to attract attention," Mydeara hissed.

"I'm over here," she said a little quieter.

Mydeara grumbled under her breath.

They followed the voice to a cage on the back of a wagon.

"I'm in here."

"We can see you," Mydeara said. "Now, shut up."

Bruce climbed up next to the cage. A beautiful brown-skinned woman brushed her long hair over her shoulder and batted her eyes. "Have you come to save me?"

"Why are you in there? Who did this to you?" asked Bruce

She pouted. "My name is Nameri. These people attacked my family's caravan and took me prisoner."

Mydeara climbed up next to him. "What do they want with you?" she asked.

"I don't know." Tears welled in her round dark eyes. "Please, set me free."

Bruce got to work on the lock, jamming his dull dagger into the keyhole.

"You look well-fed and clean. They must be taking good care of you," said Mydeara

"Oh no, they are most cruel. Please, save me." She batted her long-lashed eyes at Bruce again.

Mydeara leaned in close. "What do we get out of this if we save you?"

Bruce couldn't believe his ears. "Mydeara, that's not how a knight operates. We must save all damsels in distress. It's in the code."

"You may have noticed, Bruce, but I am not a knight, nor do I plan to be one. So, Nameri, what do we get out of the deal if we help you?"

"I'll be most grateful." She peered over their shoulders. "Are those sheep?"

Mydeara shook her head. "Observant one, aren't you? Yes, they're sheep. Now answer the question."

The lock clicked open. Bruce slowly opened the

door to the cage. "Don't mind her, Nameri. I'll save you for no cost." He shoved Mydeara aside to help the shapely woman from her cage.

"Oh thank you! You're my hero!" Nameri threw her arms around his neck and kissed him soundly on the lips.

Bruce felt himself blushing. The sheep milled around the wagon, uttering contented sounds.

A deep male voice boomed out of the darkness. "Hey there, what are you doing?"

Mydeara slipped around Nameri to stand next to Bruce, her pan ready in her hands. "Nothing," she said.

Bruce felt a sudden absence of the woman who had only seconds ago, been pressed against him. He glanced around but didn't see any sign of her. The man came closer, revealing his large arms, thick neck, and the six men who stood behind him.

"You're just standing around in our camp staring at an empty cage? Would you like to be in it?"

They both shook their heads.

Mydeara whispered, "Don't you find it odd that he's not mad about the cage being empty?"

Bruce shushed her.

Mydeara gave him an annoyed look but turned back to the seven men. "We're hungry. Do you have any food you can spare? Please?"

At that moment Bruce was thankful he'd agreed to take the girl along. Not only was she handy with her pan, she truly did look pitiful, and that very fact seemed to sway the large men accosting them.

"Why do you not eat one of these fine sheep?"

"We can't," Bruce said as he stepped forward to assert himself as leader of their little group. "They are gifts of the god Hucker and are not to be eaten."

The large man nodded. "You are wise not to anger him. One of ours did so once and now our people are doomed to wander the desert for all eternity."

"My goodness, that is a long time," said Mydeara. "What did this person do?"

"We were farmers once, with vast lands and wealth but then we became greedy and the sheep looked so tasty. We all agreed to hold a great feast. We roasted the sheep and ate them. When we woke the next morning, our lands were laid to waste, and near half our vast population lay dead in the streets. We buried them and gathered what was left, intent to go about our lives. That was not good enough for the great god Hucker." The large man gazed up at the sky and then glanced around nervously. The others behind him seemed to cower at the mention of the god's name.

"The great god Hucker came to us in the shape of one of our own, his light shown from the body he'd chosen. His being blinded us."

Bruce nodded. "We too have seen Hucker as such."

"Then you know how terrifying his presence is."

"Indeed." Though, in truth, it did not so much seem terrifying as magical. Seeing Darkious put in his place by the god had been humorous, to say the least. "What did Hucker tell you?"

"That the lands we called home would become fallow and that we were to be banished from them forevermore. And so it is that we roam the desert, always in search of a new place to call home, but never finding it."

Mydeara tapped her fingers on her frying pan. "Do you have food or not? We're starving."

"We do. I am Oskar. Come." He waved for them to follow him back to the fire.

"Say, you didn't happen to see a young woman around here, did you?" Bruce asked.

"There are plenty of young women around the fire if you desire one, brave knight."

Bruce's chest swelled within his armor. The man knew a brave knight when he saw one. As they walked toward the fire, he saw no sign of Nameri.

"Join the feast and then stay the night with us. We will be moving in the morning." Oskar indicated a table filled with platters of food and barrels of mead.

As the night wore on, women danced, men beat their drums, the singing grew louder and more off-key as barrel after barrel of mead was consumed. Bruce shifted the dead weight of Mydeara, who had passed out leaning against him, to the ground where the girl curled up with her pan and remained fast asleep.

A woman beckoned him away, offering him yet another cup of mead. He didn't need another, not that he planned to turn it down, but maybe this woman could give him some information while he was enjoying her company.

Bruce glanced at the sleeping girl. She had a good head on her shoulders and was always asking smart questions. Since she wasn't up to the task, he tried to think of something Mydeara might ask. "Where do you get all this mead if you endlessly travel the desert?"

The woman smiled. "Do you care to hear the answer or would you rather go over there?" She pointed to a blanket on the ground beside a wagon.

Bruce eyed the blanket and the cup of mead in her hand. A couple months ago, he wouldn't have thought twice about her offer. But now he'd met an evil overlord and a god. He'd seen real magic. And most of all, Nameri was out there somewhere, hopefully still nearby, and she was much prettier. If he was going to make the effort to take off his armor, knowing he was going to get sand in every conceivable crevice, it had better be for someone worthwhile. Preferably, a woman without a hulking sister to demand he marry her after the deed. Nameri clearly didn't have one of those, but this woman? He wasn't willing to risk it.

"You know what?" he said, "I just remembered I

need to—"

"Help!" Cried a familiar voice. "Oh, please help!"

Nameri needed saving again? Already? Was she really that unlucky? He began to reconsider wanting to be near her without armor. Her bad luck might get him killed.

"Is there not a brave knight who will save me?"

"Oh, shut up," said the woman with the cup of mead.

"It hurts so much. Please, someone, help me."

Bruce peered into the darkness in the direction of Nameri's voice. "I guess I should..." He nodded in that direction.

"I'm sure she's fine," said the woman.

"She doesn't sound fine," said Bruce.

"They're going to kill me. Please!"

"Sorry, duty calls." Bruce left her standing there and headed into the darkness with his sword drawn.

He slunk into the shadows, weaving in and out of the wagons and staked pack animals. The moonlight shown down on Nameri, giving her an ethereal glow where she lay tied at the wrists to the spokes of a wagon wheel. Her legs were bound as well. She writhed, more in an alluring manner than one that indicated she was in pain or frightened.

For all her 'they're going to kill me', he didn't see anyone else around. "How did you manage to get caught again so quickly? You sure managed to disappear fast when people showed up last time."

"Help. I'm bound to this wagon wheel," she said breathily.

"I can see that." He glanced around. Still finding them alone, he put his sword away. "You had plenty of opportunities to escape while we were all busy around the fire."

She sniffed. "You should have been looking for me, making sure I was safe. Not drinking and eating with everyone else."

"I thought you had escaped."

Nameri sighed. "We got interrupted last time. Let's try this again." She nodded toward the ropes around her wrists.

"Again?"

"Come on, I'll make it worth your while." She winked.

He liked the sound of that. Bruce drew his dagger and sawed through the ropes from her wrists and then her feet. "Don't run off this time."

"I don't plan to." She reached up and pulled him down onto her.

"Wait a minute. Weren't you saying that they were going to kill you? You don't want to get interrupted again, do you?"

Her tongue slid into his mouth.

He pulled away reluctantly. "We really should get you away from here so that you are not captured again."

"We'll deal with that in a minute. Please, I've

been dreaming about this for years."

He sat back. "Dreaming about what?"

She reached for him again, dragging him closer. "Being rescued by a knight in shining armor."

"It's just the moonlight. My armor is quite dinged up and highly in need of a good polishing."

"No more talking." Nameri yanked him down against her and proceeded to kiss his neck while her hands sought out the buckles of his armor.

He stayed her hand. She really was going to get him killed. "How about we get you away, find a safe place, and then you can properly thank me for rescuing you."

She sat up and glared at him. "You're ruining this for me, you know that? What happened to wanting to bed the girl? I thought that went hand in hand with the rescuing. Don't you think I'm pretty?"

"Of course."

In fact, with all the mead he'd consumed, he was having a hard time remembering why he didn't just roll with her suggestion.

"Then what's your problem? Was the rescue not dangerous enough? Do we need to do something with more risk involved?"

"You're almost making this sound like you staged the whole thing. Twice."

Nameri crossed her arms over her chest, which nearly spilled her breasts out of her low-cut shirt. "Maybe I did."

"Why would you do that?"

Tears welled in her eyes. "You've completely spoiled my dream moment." She sniffed. "I've waited for years for this and now that you're here, you had to go and wreck it."

Bruce sat back on his knees and didn't bother hiding his confusion.

"I'm a professional damsel in distress, all right? There, it's out."

"Really? I heard there were some of you out there when I was in knight school, but I never imagined meeting one of you."

She harrumphed. "Well now you have, and you've ruined everything. Her gaze focused on him with a malicious glare. "Maybe I'll ruin everything for you."

Nameri hoisted the neckline of her blouse to fully cover her breasts, jumped to her feet, and stormed off.

Not willing to stick around to find out how she planned to ruin anything, Bruce ran back to Mydeara. He tossed the sleeping girl over his shoulder, grabbed her pan, and ran into the sand with a herd of sleepy sheep trotting along behind him. He ran and ran, not caring which direction he was headed, as long as it was far from the nomads.

❧

Sunlight beat down on Bruce's eyelids. He cracked one open. His hand flew over his face, blocking out the bright rays. After giving his eyes a few moments to adjust, he turned to see Mydeara stirring beside him. The flock milled nearby.

"How are you feeling?" he asked.

The girl muttered something about mead being evil and lurched to her feet.

Bruce sat up and took in the sandy nothingness of their surroundings. Hungover himself, he dearly wished he'd had the wherewithal to grab some food during his hurried exodus. Mydeara would have thought of it. He rubbed his hands over his face, grumbling as he ended up with a grain of sand in his eye.

Mydeara turned in a slow circle "What happened to the people? The pond?"

"We had to leave quickly in the middle of the night."

"What did you do?" She gave him an accusing look then shook her head. "You know what? Nevermind. I probably don't want to know. At least we filled our water skins before we ate last night."

"There is that," he said meekly, wondering how long they could get by on only her water. He'd been too distracted to fill his own.

The ram trotted over and butted Bruce in the backside.

"I think he wants us to be on our way," said

Mydeara.

"Go on then." Bruce shooed the ram. "We might as well follow you. I have no idea where we are."

❦

Day turned to night and night into day. This succession happened for two full moon cycles before they came to a flat rocky plain of ruins. Weary beyond all-knowing, Bruce and Mydeara slumped to the ground in the shade of a crumbling wall.

"I'm about to collapse," Mydeara whispered.

"I think we already did."

"Right." She settled back against the wall and closed her eyes.

He was about to follow suit when the sheep made a mad racket. He slowly turned his head to see them gathered around a low stone wall.

"I think they found something," said Mydeara, her eyes still closed. "You go check it out. I'll wait here."

Bruce didn't want to move, but the sheep sounded more insistent by the second so he worked himself to his feet and staggered toward them.

"Water!" he shouted.

Bruce knelt by the shallow basin and dunked his head into the cool water. It felt fantastic.

Mydeara kicked him and then grimaced and rubbed her foot. "Gross. I have to drink that you know. Get your stinky, filthy head out of the water."

Bruce sat up, slicking his wet hair back. He jabbed his finger in the direction of the sheep drinking from the same water. "What about them?"

"That's different."

Too tired to argue, he filled his waterskin in silence. He wasn't going to forget this time.

The flock gnawed on the few tufts of greenery near the basin.

Mydeara watched them intently. "I'm so hungry, I could eat—"

A thready voice burst into Bruce's head. "DoOon't even think aboOoout it."

"No eating the sheep," said Bruce.

"YoOou should thank ooOour god for the water."

"Are you all right? You look pale," said Mydeara

"Thank you for the water, Hucker," he yelled to the sky, then turned back to Mydeara. "The sheep, they talk to me sometimes."

Mydeara's eyes grew wide. "Are you serious?"

"I'm afraid so. And if they get killed, they scream. Svetlana told me all about it."

Mydeara's eyes narrowed. "Who's Svetlana?"

"Why do you care?" The venom in the girl's voice put him on the defensive. Why would she be jealous anyway?"

"Nevermind." Mydeara stomped off. The sheep followed her but kept looking back at Bruce.

"Fine. I'm coming." He got back to his feet and

went after them.

After several hours of silence, Mydeara finally spoke. "So what is it that you are hoping to find at the Wall?"

He'd not thought about it too specifically. "Gold, I imagine."

"Gold is your destiny?"

"I've always wanted to be rich."

"What about being famous?"

"That too, I suppose, but fame isn't something one can just find lying at the foot of a wall."

"How long is this wall?"

"I don't know. J'hal, John, The Spawn," he shook his head. "He seemed to know about the wall, but he didn't share any actual details.

"That's handy, and his directions were so spot on. Remind me to send him a thank you note if we live through this."

"You really can't fault the kid. I mean, he finds out the life he's been living was a lie and then his real father turns up and offers him power and wealth. Who's going to turn something like that down?"

"His father is an Evil Overlord? Or have you forgotten?"

Bruce shrugged. "I didn't say the kid had a great sense of judgment."

"I don't know what I thought I saw in him."

"He did save his elf parents and their herd. Don't be so hard on yourself. I didn't think he'd turn out to be evil either."

Her face took on a pinched look. "You don't think he sent us in the wrong direction intentionally, do you?"

Bruce grimaced. "Well, he *is* evil..."

Mydeara nodded. "I suppose we should—"

A flash of light shot through the sky right above them. Bruce's first thought was that Hucker was making another appearance after being thanked for the water. But instead of a being of light, the wizard from the Evil Overlord's keep spilled out of the beam just before it vanished. He dropped to the ground, black robes billowing around him.

Mydeara's mouth dropped open. "Tim?"

❦ 15 ❦

Mydeara's Kiss

"What are you doing here? Where did you come from?" asked Bruce.

Tim straightened his uniform, brushed the dirt off, and sighed. "It's a long story."

"We're on a long walk. Feel free to share it." Bruce reached for his sword. "Last we saw you were in the employ of Darkious Maximus, Evil Overlord Extraordinaire, Master of the Nine Darknesses. Hey," he grinned, "I remembered it all."

"Yay you." Tim twirled his finger. "Not that it matters anymore."

"What does that mean?" asked Mydeara

"As of yesterday, the name to know is The Spawn of Evil Incarnate, His Highness John, the Most Dark One. We've had a change of management."

"The kid took over?" asked Bruce once he closed

his gaping mouth.

Tim nodded. "Wondering about his own mother who had been a personal secretary, the new management had a conversation with the previous management's personal secretary. He found her working conditions violated the evil union standard in countless ways. With help and encouragement from The Spawn of Evil Incarnate, His Highness John, the Most Dark One, she turned the previous management in, filing several reams worth of complaint forms. Empowered by her actions, thirty-two other staff members followed suit. Enforcers from the evil union showed up last night and took him away.

"The new managment was wise not to attempt to kill the old as I'm sure he had insurance against that very thing. Smart kid." Tim whistled appreciatively. "His father will be buried in lawsuits for the rest of his life. The evil lawyers will make sure of it."

"Wonder what kind of song old 'arold would have come up with to commemorate that," mused Mydeara. A moment later, the implications of this news began to settle in. She watched the wizard's hands carefully and started to back away.

Bruce looked worried too. "So, are you here to kill us?" he asked.

The wizard held up his empty hands. "Not at all. This is kind of an unplanned trip actually. Where might we be?"

Mydeara said, "The edge of the Desert of Despair."

"Well now, that's interesting." He stroked his goatee.

"Quit doing that." Bruce glared at Tim's chin.

"Easy habit to fall into. Sorry. I was doing a spell for The Spawn of Evil Incarnate, His Highness John, the Most Dark One, and then I found myself here."

"What spell would do that?" Mydeara asked.

"Making something disappear, apparently." He shook his head and started walking. "Just when I get a job, and a good-paying one, I might add, this has to go and happen. I swear the gods hate me."

"Why don't you just go back?"

"If it were that simple, I'd be right on it," he grumbled. "I wish it were. The new management isn't half bad. Well, evil, of course, but more fair about it. Where are you two off to?"

Bruce took his hand off his sword. "The Wall of Nok, to find my destiny."

"Sounds like as good of a plan as any," said Tim. "How many day's walk are we from the keep?"

"Try months."

"That's a long walk back alone. I suppose I'll be joining you, if you don't mind that is?"

Bruce gave the wizard a calculating look. "Can you conjure us up some food?"

"Probably wouldn't be the best idea. My conjuring has been a little off lately."

"Then I hope you enjoy a sporadic diet of cactus

and stringy rabbit," said Mydeara. "We've been wandering this whole time and have no idea where the wall is."

Tim looked up to the sky, holding up his arm and aligning it with the sun. He pursed his lips and muttered to himself. "From what I recall of the maps I've seen of this area, we can take a shortcut and be to the wall tomorrow."

"There's a shortcut?" Bruce asked.

Mydeara put her hands on her hips. "Hold on. Did The Spawn send you here to spy on us? Maybe to ensure that we died out here on our own? I mean, if we died of natural causes, Hucker couldn't do anything about it, right?"

Tim stroked his goatee. "You have a good mind about you, but no. I can honestly say, I did not plan to be here nor was I sent."

"This shortcut isn't a ploy to lead us further off track and into some planned or unplanned danger?" she asked.

"Way to cover your bases, but no."

Mydeara regarded the wizard with a sneer. "I don't like you."

"Fair enough." Tim shrugged. "The shortcut is this way. There should be berries or something around here."

As the day stretched on, Bruce asked, "I thought you said there was a shortcut."

Tim checked the setting sun. "I may have

miscalculated slightly on how long it would take to get to the shortcut, but we will get there."

Mydeara scowled. "I need those berries. Right. Now."

Tim scanned the horizon. "Hold on, let me check my map."

Mydeara let out a disgusted growl. "You have a map? What was all the checking the sky about?"

"I didn't want to use it unless I had to," Tim said with a sheepish grin. "It doesn't look near as impressive to consult a map as it does to just know where one is."

Mydeara considered killing the wizard and cooking him up. Except there was no wood in sight. Maybe she could trick him into conjuring a fire.

Tim pulled out a scroll from his sleeve and unrolled it. "Ah yes, there it is."

"Excuse me if we don't believe you," said Bruce. He brought them all to a halt as he climbed up onto a fallen stone column to survey the land. "I don't see any sign of this Wall of Nok yet. What did you say it looked like? Shouldn't I see it from here?"

Tim shook his head. "It's low lying, but a thick and sturdy wall. Not huge or spectacular in the landmark kind of sense. You'll understand when we get there. For now, though..." He eyed the sheep. "It's a shame Hucker is so attached to those sheep. I could really go for some roasted mutton about now."

The ram stepped ahead of the herd and lowered

its horns.

Mydeara clutched her growling stomach. "Us too."

Tim sighed. "I suppose I could try to conjure up something to eat. Just don't blame me if it goes wrong."

The wizard looked awfully nervous for *supposing* anything. He walked off a way. Mydeara stayed put, feeling safer at a distance.

There was a flash of light and what sounded like a clap of thunder that made her jump. A smoky haze filled the air where Tim had been standing.

An unfamiliar voice called out, "Oh wow, like a real knight!"

The haze cleared to reveal Tim and a clean-shaven young man in strange clothes that hadn't been there a few seconds ago. Tim appeared flushed, and his smile was clearly forced.

"Who are you?" she asked, coming closer.

"Barry." He winked. "What's your name?"

"Mydeara." She felt herself blushing.

Bruce clanged his way over to Tim. "Who is this boy and where did he come from?"

"This dude grabbed me out of my basement," said Barry, jutting his chin toward Tim.

Bruce scowled. "You have a strange way of speaking."

"So do you. Good thing we all speak common," said Barry.

"What is 'common'?" Mydeara asked.

"You know, the language. Common means we can all easily understand each other even though we come from different places."

"And just where did *you* come from?" Bruce asked as he looked Barry up and down.

Tim let out a nervous laugh. "I did say my magic was a bit off, didn't I?"

"You conjured him?" Mydeara asked. "Wrong kind of berry, Tim." She clutched her pan, lining up a shot with Tim's head. "You were supposed to conjure food! We're all going to starve out here!"

Tim eyed Mydeara's pan nervously.

"What, are we supposed to eat Barry?" asked Bruce, looking every bit as hungry and frustrated as she felt.

She had to admit, Barry might not be on a bush, but she wouldn't mind nibbling on him. Younger than Bruce, more the age of The Spawn but without the evil overlord father. Barry smiled at her, his blue eyes sparkling through strange round lenses.

"You wouldn't eat me, would you?" He looked between them, holding up his hands and backing away.

"I'm not quite ready to turn to cannibalism just yet," Bruce said.

"Good." Barry looked around. "What is this place?"

Mydeara said, "The Desert of Despair, land of

ruins, rubble and graves."

"It's awesome. This is way better than my stepmom's basement. That's where I live," he said, grinding the toe of his shoe into the sand. "I mean I have a job and stuff. I'm not some loser."

A nice boy with a job didn't sound bad at all. Mydeara smiled. In fact, it sounded like exactly what she'd been looking for since she'd left home.

"Can you send him back?" asked Bruce.

Tim closed his eyes and dropped his head to his chest. "I wish I could. I mean, I could, but who knows what would go wrong with that?"

"What do you mean?" asked Barry.

"I mean, I haven't cast a spell right almost five months."

"Not that I'm in a rush to leave, but what do you think would straighten out your spell abilities?" Barry asked.

"I don't know."

"Well, when my RPG mage gets in a bind, he has to hunt down new spell books." Barry cocked his head, staring off into the distance. "This one time my mage had to find a beautiful girl and get her to kiss him to break the curse that had been put upon him."

Tim gestured to the surrounding ruins. "Bit of a shortage on books and women at the moment."

"Hey, hello?" shouted Mydeara. "If it might mean we'd get a meal, I'll kiss him."

"Are you sure about this, Mydeara?" Bruce asked,

while simultaneously shoving her at Tim.

She'd much rather have kissed Barry, but he couldn't conjure food. And she was starving. "Are you sure this will work?" she asked.

"No, but it wouldn't hurt to try," said Barry. "If we had another wizard around, he could work his magic on Tim, but we don't."

Tim nodded. "I was hoping to get the evil overlord to help me, but thanks to the management change, I didn't get a chance. How is it that you know a fair amount about magic?

Barry pushed the glasses up on his nose. "I read a lot of books."

"Spell books?"

"No. Gamer books. Dungeon master guides, that sort of thing."

"I have no idea what you are talking about."

"Look old dude, how much mana do you have?"

"What?"

"Magic power. You know."

"It's not something I can measure."

"Really? Don't they give you your stats when you leave your trainer?"

"My mentor?"

"Whatever, yeah." Barry rolled his eyes. "You're hopeless, old dude. What kind of name is Tim anyway? It doesn't sound real medieval."

"What is this medieval? You have so many strange words." Tim shook his head. "My name is

Timininious. Darkious Maximus, Evil Overlord Extraordinaire, Master of the Nine Darknesses deemed me Tim.

"Oh dude, that's funny. Have you ever seen... nevermind, of course, you haven't. For lack of other options, let's try the kiss." Barry stepped toward Mydeara.

Bruce cleared his throat. "You mean between Mydeara and Tim."

"Right. Yes." Barry scuttled out of the way.

Mydeara drew a deep breath and let it out. "Nothing funny, wizard, and keep your hands to yourself."

Tim nodded solemnly.

Here goes nothing, she thought as she closed her eyes and leaned in. Her lips met with Tim's, dry and awkward, touching but unmoving for fear of making it any more intimate than the kiss needed to be.

There, their lips had touched. Did that make it a kiss? Did it need to be passion-filled to count? Did teeth need to be explored, tongues intertwined for it to be counted as a real kiss? Did she need to think about it other than the mere act of touching his lips or did it become a kiss simply by the fact that their lips had touched? What part of that made it magic, if truly there was any magic to be had in a kiss?

"All right, enough of that," Bruce bellowed.

Mydeara stepped back.

Tim pursed his lips and furrowed his brow. "I

don't feel any different."

Mydeara wiped her mouth on her sleeve.

"Try a spell," urged Barry.

"Give me a moment to think. I don't want to pull anyone else from who knows where. Let's see if I can find something mundane." Tim closed his eyes and muttered to himself.

Mydeara looked around, wondering what it was that he'd tried to do. No flashes of light or undead frogs popped into existence. But she smelled something, something good. Her mouth watered. She inhaled deeply and turned around. A platter of steaming haunches of meat circled with potatoes sat on the ground behind her.

"Food! Tim, you've done it!" She ran over and hugged the wizard.

"I have?"

She stepped aside to reveal the platter.

"My aim still seems to be off." He raised an eyebrow. "You wouldn't perchance be interested in another kiss to fine-tune things?"

"Not a chance. But thank you for the meal."

He bowed. "And thank you for the kiss."

Bruce had already set upon the platter with great gusto. Mydeara grabbed a haunch of meat and took a bite. Juices ran down her chin. It tasted glorious."

"What even is that?" Barry asked, peering over her shoulder.

"I don't care," she said while chewing.

Once her stomach was filled, she sat on a rock and watched the three men finish off the platter of meat and potatoes. What were her father and brother eating without her home to cook for them? She realized she'd barely given her family thought since she'd left the village, but now she dearly missed them. Maybe it was because Barry was also far from home. Though he still seemed to be wrapped up in the adventure of it all.

Bruce, being a knight, would always be off on a quest and she'd thought that sounded exciting when they'd met, but now, she missed her bed and knowing where her next meal would come from. Not that she minded adventure, but she'd had an awful lot of them since she'd left home. A little break would be nice. A little break with Barry would be even better.

He glanced up just then to catch her smiling at him and blushed.

He said he had a job, and he seemed to know about magic. As long as he wasn't a knight or a wizard, he had promise.

"What do you do, Barry?" she asked.

"I work in the kitchen at Burger Hut. I know that's not very exciting, but the food is pretty good and the pay isn't awful."

"You like to cook?"

He nodded.

"Me too." She held up her pan.

"You carry a pan with you?"

Bruce chuckled. "And you best watch out for it. She's got a wicked aim with that thing and a powerful swing. It's quite impressive. You should have seen her attacking goblins," he said proudly.

His compliment made her smile.

Barry's eyes lit up. "Real goblins?"

Why was he so excited about goblins? "They killed a lot of people."

"This is better than being on a movie set! Can we see them?"

"Hopefully not," said Bruce. "Now that The Spawn is the new evil overlord, we'll have to see what his plans are."

"One of his first orders was to return the corpse frogs I'd created back to the swamp where they live. Something about an endangered species and preserving the natural order of the swamp. So whatever you do, don't wander there," said Tim.

"Corpse frogs?" Barry shook his head, grinning. "I wonder how many hit points a real goblin has. Wait, Mydeara, you attacked them with your pan?"

"I'm a girl, silly, we don't get sword training. We have to make do with what we have."

"Right, I forgot about the whole inequality thing." He nodded. "That is so cool that you attacked goblins with a pan. What did it sound like?"

"The goblins? Some screamed at me. Others fell to the ground without a sound. The really scary part was the troll."

"Oh man! A troll? That's killer!"

"That's what we thought too," Mydeara said. "It tried to kill Bruce but then J'hal showed up and we got away." As they all finished eating, Mydeara filled Barry in on the rest of their adventures.

When she'd finished, she realized Bruce and Tim had left the two of them alone. She spotted them a ways off with the flock nearby. Bruce gave her an impatient look.

He could wait a few more minutes.

"Enough about me," she said. "What do you do for fun?"

"Nothing cool like you." He grinned. "I play video games, play RPGs with my friends, and watch movies."

"I don't know what any of that means."

"That's all right." Barry patted her on the shoulder. "I like you more because you don't. This place is way better than where I come from."

"They're waiting for us. Come on." She held out her hand and was happy when Barry took it and didn't let go as they walked.

"Tim, will you be able to send Barry home now that your magic is fixed?" she asked when they joined the others.

"Maybe." He stroked his goatee. "Since I didn't intentionally cast the spell to remove him from wherever he was, it will be tricky sending him back."

Barry asked, "Can't you just trace the threads of

magic?"

"I don't know what tomes you've been reading boy, but you've got some crazy notions."

"According to Tim's map, we're close. We should get moving," said Bruce.

Barry walked along in silence, sticking close to Mydeara's side.

She glanced over at him. He seemed sad. "He'll figure out a way to send you back."

"Maybe I don't want to go home. Tell me about your home first, and then I'll decide."

Mydeara described her village, her home, and her brother and father.

"That doesn't sound so bad. Are you a good cook?"

"My father says I am."

"She is." Bruce smiled at her. "She cooked me a fine meal before I left the village."

Barry shot Bruce a jealous glare. Mydeara grinned, thinking that her adventure might just have taken a very welcome turn.

❧ 16 ❧

Barry Takes A Flying Leap

Barry regarded the dark tunnel in the looming mountain with trepidation. "We're going in there?"

"If we want to get to the Wall of Nok, then yes." Tim trudged onward down the rocky pathway.

Mydeara's fingers intertwined with his. He squeezed her hand and tried to sound confident as he said, "I'm sure it will all be fine."

She muttered something about the wizard being an employee of an untrustworthy evil overlord, but she followed him into the gaping hole all the same.

Inside, the light from the opening faded and his eyes adjusted to the darkness. "What is this place?"

"Ancient dwarven mines," said Tim.

"Oh cool!" His pulse pounded. "I wish the guys from home could see this. It's like right out of that novel about the hobbit and the ring."

Tim turned to him. "You know of hobbits?"

Feeling caught on the spot, all the knowledge he'd gleaned from reading the entire series of books slipped from his mind. "Only a little."

· "Little. Ha!" Tim laughed.

Bruce shook his head. "Ugh. That was bad."

Barry let his unintentional pun hang in the dank air and concentrated on not falling on his face in front of Mydeara. His luck, he'd slip and break his glasses and then he'd be screwed. It was bad enough he had to compete with a wizard and a knight for her attention. Bumbling about blind wouldn't help him one bit.

"Everyone stand back," said Tim. "I'm going to try a light spell. I don't want to set you on fire."

"No arguments here," Bruce said, urging Tim to walk ahead of them into the complete blackness.

A couple of lines of muttering later, a golden light flickered, floating just above Tim's butt.

The wizard spun around twice, looking like a dog chasing his tail. "Where is it?"

"Your behind is glowing," Bruce said, snickering.

Tim trudged into the mines, grumbling about his aim still being off. The flock followed behind Bruce, Tim's light reflecting in their round eyes. When they came to a long rickety rope bridge that hung precariously over a deep chasm, Bruce shook his head.

"I'm not crossing that," said the knight. "My

armor is too heavy. And how do you expect the flock to traverse that thing?"

"Oh, we're not crossing it, don't worry. I told you there was a shortcut."

"This tunnel isn't it?" asked Mydeara.

"No. Well, sort of, but not exactly."

"He does sound like a wizard," Barry whispered to Mydeara. "Or maybe a dragon. Neither of them speaks plainly. Or so I've read."

"Bruce met a dragon. He could tell you. The dragon is part of his main quest."

Barry's heart hammered in his chest. Dragons were real too? If this was a dream, he hoped he didn't wake up until the quest was over and he got the girl. He hoped he got the girl. She was epically awesome, like a character right out of a fantasy novel.

"Just follow me," said Tim. He walked to the edge of the chasm and stepped off.

"What are you doing?" yelled Mydeara.

"Tim!" shouted Bruce.

They all ran to the edge. Tim's robes fluttered about as he plummeted downward, taking their light with him. And then he was gone. The mine instantly turned black.

Every sound was suddenly amplified. Barry could hear Mydeara breathing fast, the hooves of the flock shuffling on stone, and Bruce's armor creaking. But the wizard hadn't even screamed.

"He didn't hit the bottom," said Mydeara.

She was right. They hadn't heard a thud, a splat, nothing to indicate he'd hit the ground. Maybe there wasn't ground to hit. Maybe it was an endless chasm. A world with goblins, dragons, and evil overlords would undoubtedly have such a thing.

"We're supposed to follow him?" Bruce asked.

"That's what he said, but I don't know about jumping off the edge," said Mydeara.

"Really? You're sure?" asked Bruce.

"You heard him," said Mydeara.

"No, not you. The sheep said we should jump."

Barry began to reevaluate Bruce's sanity. He whispered to Mydeara, "Bruce talks to the sheep?"

"I think it's more that they talk to him, but yes," she said.

A talking dragon was one thing, but sheep? Barry shook his head.

The sheep seemed to move all at once, creating a racket. And then there was silence.

"Did they just—" asked Barry.

"Go over the edge? Yes," said Bruce. "Might as well follow. We'd probably break our necks trying to go anywhere else in this pitch-black mine."

Bruce's armor clanked. "Wheeeeeeeeeeee," he shouted until his voice faded and then was suddenly gone.

Mydeara tugged at his hand. "Come on then. Just walk forward. We'll hit the edge."

She went over half a step before him, pulling

him with her. Tim and even the sheep had remained quiet. Bruce had made the fall sound like fun. They were all crazy. Barry screamed.

Then he hit the ground. He expected a jolt that would shatter every bone in his body, but it was more like he'd tripped over his foot. He landed on a soft carpet of lush grass. Mydeara was already on her feet, brushing herself off.

He scrambled up, looking around to see everyone else had made it safely to...wherever they were.

"Were you screaming?" asked Bruce.

"No," Barry said quickly.

Mydeara gave him a look but didn't say anything.

"So where's this wall?" asked Bruce.

Tim pointed to a long stretch of stones stacked waist-high. It went on as far as he could see in either direction.

"That's it?" asked Bruce.

Tim nodded. "Nok was a dwarf. It's a fairly high wall for his kind.

Barry pondered the line of haphazardly stacked rocks. "I expected something more, I don't know, monumental." Something more like The Great Wall of China or that Berlin wall he'd read about in history class.

The sheep frolicked in the long grass. "They look happy," he said.

Mydeara nodded. "This is the first time I've seen them this happy. Bruce, are they saying anything?"

The knight squinted at the sheep. "They said, CoOoongratulatioOoons."

Barry laughed. "Do they really talk like that?"

"Would I make that up?"

He might. Barry barely knew the knight for goodness' sake, but in the spirit of keeping things happy after all falling through a dark chasm, he didn't argue the point. "So what are we looking for here?"

"His destiny," Mydeara said in his ear.

"And what might that look like?"

She shrugged. "What should we do, Bruce?"

"I suggest we spread out," said Tim.

Bruce scowled. "I'm sure you do. You want to find my destiny. But you can't have it. It's mine. You all sit here and wait for me. I'm going to go find it."

Tim shrugged and sat down in the grass. "Fine. Be that way. I'll sit back here and enjoy a rest."

Mydeara pulled Barry down next to her, her fingers toying with his. She looked into his eyes and blushed.

Thoughts of his future raced through his mind. "If I were to stay here, what kind of job could I get?"

"You'd stay?" Her eyes grew moist. "Really?"

Staying here sounded way better than a future of trying to save up enough money to buy a car and a place of his own by working at Burger Hut. He nodded.

She threw her arms around his neck and kissed

him. "My father runs a store. I'm sure you could work for him. My brother is too young to be of much use. Maybe someday, if we save up some coin, we could open an inn of our own. Think of the meals we could cook together."

Meals were the last thing on his mind. "Sure, sounds great."

Bruce interrupted the dreams of his future with Mydeara by barging back into their midst.

"That was fast," said Tim.

Bruce held something large and transparent in his hands. "I found it! I found my destiny!"

Barry jumped up to get a better look. "Looks like a giant crystal. Those things go for hundreds of dollars back home. But this one is so round and polished." He whistled. "I bet you could get a grand out of that easy."

Bruce's face took on a pinched look. "Sure, if you say so. Now I just have to get it home so I can show it off and gain my fame before selling it to gain my riches."

"Oh Bruce, I'm so happy for you." Mydeara got to her feet and hugged the knight.

Tim jumped to his feet, his eyes wide. He pointed a shaking finger at the crystal. "*That* is your destiny?"

Bruce nodded, proudly holding his treasure.

"Keep that thing away from me. I just finally got my magic working again. Wait, let me touch it. Maybe this time... No. Nevermind." He gave the crystal one last look before letting out a deep sigh. "Well then, I'm happy to announce that, thanks to the lovely Mydeara, I can save us all a lot of walking, and we don't even have to go over a cliff this time. As a parting gift, before I return to find out if I still have a job, I will teleport you all to Mydeara's village."

"You're all right, Tim." Bruce clapped the wizard on the shoulder.

The wizard grimaced and pulled out his map. "If you could just point me to your village, I'll get working on the spell."

Mydeara peered at the map, finally pointing to a dot near what looked like a sea or ocean. Someone had drawn a head in the water with a puddle of green next to it.

"Is that head throwing up?" Barry asked.

Bruce shuddered. "The Sea of Sickness. I'm not looking forward to that part of the voyage."

"We're not sailing that are we?" Barry asked Mydeara.

"Not on your life." She turned to Tim. "Maybe put us a bit away from the village? What with your aim being off an all?"

"A sound suggestion, Mydeara." Tim raised his hands to the sun and began to chant. The flock gathered around Bruce. "It was, well, eventful, knowing you all." He waved his hands with a flourish.

Everything around Barry grew impossibly bright and then suddenly he, Mydeara, Bruce, and the flock stood in a vast field of wheat. A quaint village sat at the bottom of the hill, filled with people going about their business.

"Come on," Mydeara took his hand and pulled him along. "I can't wait for you to meet my family."

❦ 17 ❦

Svetlana's Surprise

Svetlana peered at the path leading into the village from the grasslands. She heard voices, voices that didn't belong to any beasts or mysterious creatures. Human voices. Her heart leapt. Then there he was, his armor slightly more dented than before, but there was no mistaking the knight. Brucey had returned.

She stroked her belly. How was she going to explain that? She didn't know, but she ran into the grass to meet him.

"You came back!" She threw her arms around his neck and kissed him soundly. "I knew you would."

Bruce smiled weakly, shifting the wrapped object he carried to his other arm. "Yeah, about that."

"Come back to the village and tell me all about it. You must be hungry and tired." She tugged at his hand, noticing his missing arm plate. "What happened to your armor?"

"I'll explain later." He turned around "We're here, hurry it up."

Behind him, a young couple and a flock of sheep came into view.

"You still have the sheep." She patted his cheeks. "That makes me so happy. Who are those two?"

"Friends. So umm, what's that?" His voice cracked as he pointed at her swelling belly.

She knew he'd notice. But she wasn't prepared to answer so soon. "Can we sit and talk first?"

Bruce cringed. "Yes, I suppose so." His pace seemed to slow but he plodded onward.

The ground shook with familiar thundering footsteps. The female troll slid to a stop just shy of slamming into the wall of the building beside Svetlana.

"Jonquil, what have I told you about running in the village?"

"Sorry," the troll trilled in her high-pitched voice. "I saw there were strangers and I missed clearing them before they made it here. How did you do that?" She directed the last line to the three humans surrounded by sheep.

Jonquil's gaze flitted over all of them and then settled on Bruce. She grinned, baring her large square teeth. "You came back! Where did your glorious pelt go?"

Bruce looked utterly terrified. He grabbed the

shoulder of the girl beside him who held a pan in her hands as if ready to do battle.

Svetlana clapped, drawing the troll's attention back to her. "He can't understand you, remember? And he's mine. We have an agreement."

The troll's wide shoulders slumped. "Yes. You have his baby."

"That's right. He's mine. Now go on. I think we're safe enough for now. I'll see that you get extra food tonight."

"Thank you, Svetlana. You are most kind."

The troll gave Bruce a longing look as she stomped out of the village with her tiny wings drooping behind her.

"Was that a troll?" asked the boy with Bruce.

The girl nodded. "We've met before. Are you all right there, Bruce? Need a change of pants or anything?"

Bruce cleared his throat but his voice still came out strangled. "I'm fine."

"Jonquil's nothing to worry about," said Svetlana. "I met her on one of my walks. She was lonely and needed a job. We women have to help each other out." She gave the girl a meaningful look. "Jonquil has been doing a wonderful job of dealing with the goblin problem as well as local ruffians and crooked merchants. In return, we provide her with a house at the edge of the village and free meals."

"How do you understand her?" asked Bruce.

"Oh, it was a gift, like how I could talk to the sheep," she said.

"The village has been safe since I left?" asked the girl.

"Safe, yes. You're from here?" Something about the girl's face tickled Svetlana's memory. "You wouldn't be Mydeara, the girl who went missing months ago, would you? There were lost girl posters all around the village for weeks."

Mydeara wilted. She glanced at Bruce. "I never got around to sending a message back home to let them know I was safe."

Bruce patted her arm. "I'm sure your family will be happy to see you. And hey, you have that adventure to tell your future kids about."

Mydeara grinned. "That I do."

Svetlana led the travelers to the new Sheep's Inn she'd had built since Brucey had left. "What do you think?" She pointed to the two-story building with the sign bearing a smiling sheep out front.

"It looks just like your dad's place," he said.

"Do you think he'd be proud of it?"

"Does it make money?"

"Oh yes. We've been pretty booked up."

"Then he'll be quite proud." He turned to his traveling companions. "Do you two need a room? You've been ogling each other since Barry stepped out of the smoke."

"We have not," huffed Mydeara. "But no, thank

you. We're going to see my father. I'm sure we can find somewhere for Barry to sleep until we make things official."

The boy nodded toward Svetlana's belly. "I think you're going to be making things official before we are."

"Go on then," Bruce growled. "I'll look for you before I leave the village."

The couple ran off hand in hand.

Svetlana guided Bruce inside. The large main room was filled with people talking, eating, and drinking. A filled dining hall was her favorite sound. She checked to make sure the staff were all working and then turned back to Bruce.

He glanced around with a seeming look of dread. "Where's your sister?"

"Olga? She's at home."

"She went back to Holden and left you here all alone?"

He did still care! She could see the concern in his eyes. Her heart swelled. "No silly, she married Bjorn the blacksmith shortly after you left. Her home is here."

"Married? Olga? That had to be a sight to see."

She knew the two of them didn't get along, but it hurt her to hear the barbs the two tossed back and forth. "She's really quite happy."

"That would also be a sight to see. I'm sure they'll make giant babies together. Though, I suppose, if she's happy, maybe she's in a better mood?"

"Oh yes, she most certainly is." She couldn't resist giving him a peck on the cheek. "How about a bath and then I'll get you something to eat. I can get you a room of your own, or you can share mine." She batted her eyes.

He eyed her belly again. "I think we've shared quite enough, haven't we?"

"Can't do any harm now, can it?"

He rubbed his hands over his face. "How about the bath and the meal and about six cups of strong ale, then I'll decide."

"Anything for you, my dear."

She led him to the room off the dining hall where the bathing tub sat and closed the door, sliding the bolt into place. She pumped the handle until water started to flow.

"I don't suppose you have any warm water?" he asked.

"Bjorn came up with the idea of running metal pipes behind his furnace so the water is heated. A little anyway."

She helped him out of his armor, reminding her of the time they'd shared on the ship when they'd been so happy together.

Once he'd gotten into the water, she gave him a good scrubbing. Then she let him soak for a bit while she sent his clothes off to be laundered and found some for him to wear in the meantime. When he was dried and dressed, she ordered two meals and a small cask of ale be brought up to her room. She also had one of the staff deliver his armor to her room. Bruce held a large object wrapped in a cloth-like it was his most prized possession. He followed her up the stairs.

"Did you find what you were looking for?"

"I think so, yeah. Do you want to see it?"

She nodded.

Once they were inside her room and the door was closed, he unwrapped a crystal bigger than her head.

Svetlana gasped. "That's beautiful. It's got to be worth a fortune."

"I'm hoping so. Do you think your father would want to buy it?"

"He might. If he doesn't, I bet he would know of someone who would."

A knock at the door brought two bowls of steaming stew, a loaf of bread, and the ale. Bruce grabbed the bread, ripped it in half, and shoved an end into the bowl. He took a big bite and closed his eyes, chewing contentedly. She poured them each a cup of ale and sat down to join him.

"You have no idea how much I've missed stew. It's just not a good on the road kind of meal, taking hours to prepare, you know?"

"I do." Svetlana joined him in a contented sigh. The man knew the value of a good meal and appreciated the long hours she slaved over her signature stew. Without her sheep to serve in it, she'd had to resort to goat, but the flavor still worked and these folks didn't know any different. They'd never tasted her holy sheep stew. Now that Brucey was back with the sheep, they could get to work on that new holy woolen clothing line they'd talked about. And all the other plans for their future she'd suggested when they sailed the boat to Gambreland. He'd been so agreeable then, laying beside her, as if he'd grant her every wish just to be with her again.

He paused mid-chew, talking around the contents in his mouth. "Speaking of cooking, would you do me a favor?"

She waited for him to finish his bite before nodding. Time on the road had made his manners atrocious. "Perhaps."

"Those two kids that traveled with me. They'd be a good fit for your kitchen and they'll need jobs if they plan to make a life for themselves here."

Pleased he was thinking of business, Svetlana nodded. "Consider it done."

His smile made her all warm and tingly inside. She figured there was no better time to broach the topic that might be heavy on his mind.

"I know you're wondering about the child I carry." She laid a protective hand on her belly.

Bruce nodded apprehensively, shoving another bite in his mouth.

"When you left..." she sniffed, remembering how broken-hearted she'd been when the days stretched into a week. Olga had told her over and over that Bruce wasn't coming back but she wanted so badly to believe her sister was wrong. She'd traveled out into the grasslands looking for him every day for weeks.

"You didn't come back. I didn't know what to think."

Bruce chewed his stew and wiped the edge of the bowl with a piece of bread.

"Brucey, I...I don't know how to tell you this but this baby—"

He sighed as if all the air had left his body. "Fine. I slept with you. It's obvious the babe is mine. Gods and surprises." He laughed ruefully. "I'll see you home and see that you're cared for. I'd be a lousy knight if I didn't own up to my mis—"

"So you'll come home with me?"

"Of course."

She leapt from her seat and kissed him. It wasn't his child, she had that on very high authority, but how could she tell him that when he offered to take care of her? It would make things so much easier to go home if she had Bruce, the knightly hero at her side. No one would question the baby when Bruce revealed the crystal. Daddy would see how wonderful he was then.

✨ 18 ✨

Destiny Finds Bruce

Bruce, glad to once again be on solid ground and several pounds lighter thanks to the weeks of seasickness, walked into Holden with Svetlana at his side. She appeared no worse for the sea voyage. Maybe the pregnancy had helped her somehow. Olga followed behind them, having left her husband in Gambreland to manage the inn in their absence.

The Holden Sheep's Inn looked much like it had before, other than the extreme silence filling the air. Shuffling footsteps caught his ear. He held his treasure close and peered around. "Is someone here?"

Gildersnorf popped his head out of the half-open door. "You finally came back?" His fist shook in the air. Grey hairy eyebrows hung low over his angry eyes. "Do you have any idea what kind of terror we've lived under while you and my daughters were sightseeing over in Gambreland? People have died! Great numbers of them!"

Bruce took a step back. "We weren't exactly sightseeing, you know. Svetlana was busy setting up a new inn."

Svetlana lurched forward, her bulging stomach making its debut. "We're home now, Daddy!"

"Nooooo! Why, I'll kill you!" The dwarf surged toward Bruce, pulling an axe from his belt.

Bruce took another step back. How was he supposed to make peace with her father while he was holding an axe? Fighting the dwarf also didn't seem like a good plan.

Gildersnorf swung the axe up into the air, ready to strike.

Bruce held his treasure behind his back with one hand and did a quick check of his chest plate, that being as high as the dwarf could reach, and found everything in order. He braced himself for the impact.

Tears filled Svety's eyes. "Stop! Daddy, Brucey is not the father."

"What?" Bruce and Gildersnorf said at the same time.

Olga strode forward to stand between them. "Daddy, it's true, Svety is not carrying Bruce's child."

Even hearing it a second time, Bruce couldn't believe his ears.

"You...lied to me? You let me believe I was the father?" he sputtered.

"And you'll thank me for it!" she said. "Or perhaps you'd find Jonquil more to your liking? The only reason she stuck around the village instead of chasing after you was because I told her you were the father of my child."

"Oh. Well, umm, thank you then, I guess." Now he was off the hook in the father department and he'd evaded the love-sick troll. Bruce sighed with great relief.

Gildersnorf did not lower his blade. He dodged around Olga and stalked toward Bruce. "I charged you with keeping my daughters safe while they were under your watch." He pointed at Svetlana's rotund stomach. "I don't call that safe."

Bruce attempted to collect his wits. "For as long as your daughters were in my charge, I kept them safe. That included protecting Svetlana from the captain during our initial voyage. We had to stop production of the sheep. Though I can see how this particular solution might not be agreeable to you." He took another step back. "After that, we had a parting of ways upon arriving in Gambreland. We had separate reasons for being there. You knew that before we set off. You didn't expect me to drag your daughters to the Wall of Nok and back, did you?"

"I expected you to keep them safe on your knight's honor."

People put so much stock in one single line within the knight's code. One line out of three hundred, and a sublet of another line even. Not at all significant on its own. Yet, this *knight's honor* seemed to weigh heavy on everyone's view of a knight. Perhaps when he continued on with his coin purse filled with gold, he'd travel back to the knight school and see about having the line amended.

"I expected my daughters to arrive home in the same condition that they left it."

"But, Daddy," Olga bent down to lay a hand on his arm. "I'm happy to not be in the condition I was when we left. Look at me."

Bruce joined Gildersnorf in giving the eldest sister a good once over.

She'd lost much of her manly appearance, her curves taking more prominence than her muscles. Wearing a nice dress and having her hair done up helped matters too. She was still a large girl, but not one that he'd imagine swinging a sword around. Though, he knew she still did, but her sword was currently packed away.

Gildersnorf didn't grin. He scowled. "You've lost your touch, girl! Lost it and your sister's virtue! How could you?"

Svetlana knelt by her father. "It's all right Daddy. The sheep are much happier now. Did you know that they screamed every time we killed them?"

"They are sheep, you stupid girl! I don't imagine

anything is happy to be killed."

"Daddy, they aren't just sheep, they are god-gifted sheep. We were killing them, angering Hucker, the sheep god, and depleting his flock with each sheep that went into the stew pot. We're very fortunate that he favored me so highly."

"Speaking of those sheep, I suppose they are all gone now?" He dropped his arm, his axe hanging by his side. "I guess that means we'll be needing to change the name of the inns and all the interior decorating, the theme song, the table centerpieces your mother worked so hard on. This renovation is going to come out of your paycheck, Svety."

"Daddy, wait," Svetlana explained their exclusive holy woolen clothing line idea.

Gildersnorf rubbed a hand through his beard. "That just might work." He eyed up his youngest daughter. "Is there something else you'd like to tell me?"

Her chin rose and she looked him in the eye. "Daddy, I'm going to have a baby."

"I sort of figured that part out, silly girl. I meant who has become your husband?"

"Oh, that." Svetlana got to her feet. "Did Olga tell you that she got married? She found the nicest blacksmith. She and Bjorn are so happy together."

Gildersnorf kept his gaze locked on his youngest daughter. "Svetlana, who is the father of this child?"

"I'm not at liberty to say exactly. I can tell you that

this child will bring us back into favor with Hucker and bring his blessing down upon us."

Gildersnorf huffed. "Bring shame upon us all, you mean. Unwed trollop!"

Svetlana cleared her throat loudly. "Brucey, wouldn't you like to show Daddy what you found at the Wall of Nok?

"Sure." Seeing the tenuous situation about ready to explode yet again, Bruce pulled the crystal from his pack. "Quite a find, isn't it?"

Gildersnorf's eyes grew wide. "That's huge! My family told a story to me when I was a child about a crystal called the God's Eye that they'd found deep within the mountain mines. I thought it was only a rumor."

Bruce held his treasure up to the sun.

Prisms danced on the white wall of the inn. One ended up on Gildersnorf's nose. Olga laughed.

"Now, *that* is sure to bring the favor of the gods upon us!" Gildersnorf exclaimed.

A great fluttering filled the sky above them. A scream emanated from two streets over, reminding Bruce of his last visit to the city. "That's not the—"

"Dragon!" yelled a man as he ran down the street with his arms clasped overtop his head. "Run for your lives!"

Gildersnorf stared upward. "I'm going to leave you to deal with this one, Bruce. It's about time you did. Everyone else, inside!" He held the door open and waved his daughters into the lobby. The door slammed shut.

Bruce took a look around. Everyone else had vanished too. Not a sound other than wing beats buffeting his ears. He sighed. No need to draw his sword and put on a good show. There wasn't an audience to care. Not that he'd needed it before either, but just once, he'd have liked the chance to do battle with a dragon. Showing up at knight school with a dragon trophy might add some weight to his request to do away with that silly knight's honor line.

He shifted his treasure to one hand and hid it behind his back. He held up the other hand to protect his face from the dirty wind the dragon's wings kicked up as it tumbled to a landing in front of him. The massive creature fumbled and rolled. Bruce peeked through his fingers.

The dragon sat up against the wall of the inn, heaving and panting, droplets of sweat running down its head. "So. You. Are. Back," it heaved.

Bruce put his hand down and nodded. "It seems so." The dragon had nearly doubled in size, making him think of Svetlana. A thought chilled him. "You're not going to lay eggs, are you?"

The dragon glared at him. "I'll have you know, I'm a male dragon. I don't know what they teach you louts at that pathetic knight school these days, but male dragons don't lay eggs. Did you really not even know I was a male?"

"Sorry, no, it's not like I can tell by your voice, and I wasn't checking out your anatomy the last time we spoke."

"Fair enough. Did you find it?"

Bruce kept the crystal behind his back. "Find what?"

"What you sought at the Wall of Nok?"

"I suppose so. Old Herman, the seer, died before he could tell me anything other than I'd find what I sought."

"Adventure?"

"Yes, there was a good deal of that."

"Beautiful women?"

Bruce thought a moment. "There were a few."

"Glory?"

"A little." Bruce smiled.

"Gold?"

He felt for his money purse, a couple coins within jangled together in a most pathetic show of wealth. "Not really."

"Shame. All successful quests should end in a heap of gold."

"I did get to meet a god. I suppose that counts for something."

The dragon snorted. "Doesn't exactly pay the bills though, does it?"

Bruce's shoulders slumped a little. "Not really." Sick of being torn down by the dragon, he decided to change the topic. "Put on a little weight, haven't you?"

The dragon patted his belly. "Seems there are lots of thieves in this town."

"Did you ever find your treasure that was stolen?"

"No. I haven't come across the particular thief that stole my treasure. Yet."

"I suppose that accounts for your girth and the lack of townsfolk."

The dragon nodded and let out a contented belch. "So, what do you have behind your back?"

Bruce gulped. If he lost this crystal, he'd have nothing, even less than he'd first come into this town with. "Just a trinket. Something I picked up at the gift shop at the Wall of Nok."

The dragon clapped. "I do so love souvenirs. That's why I'm so upset over having this one stolen. I'd had it for over three hundred years, ever since my travels to the Dwarven Mines." His eyes took on a far way look. "Such beautiful rainbows. I swear I caught a glimpse of them just moments ago."

Bruce inhaled sharply, near choking on his spit. He coughed. "I wonder who the thief might have been. You say it was taken from you while you were here?"

The dragon rolled toward him, floundering on its feet. "Yes, I was taking a nap in my cave with my pretty crystal in my hands. When I woke up, it was gone. I'm a light sleeper so I'm not sure how the thief managed it. I've been rather upset about that as well."

Bruce sighed, knowing what he had to do to save the town and yet hating it at the same time. He held out the crystal. "Did it look like this?"

The dragon lunged forward, grabbing the crystal with his talons. "You found it!" He danced around, shaking the buildings near them with every hop. Clay shingles fell to the cobbles, shattering into tiny shards. Cracks snaked up the walls of the inn and all the other buildings surrounding them.

"Yes, it seems so. Could you calm down just a little, please?"

"Oh, thank you!" The dragon grinned, exposing its sharp, long teeth. "You truly are a most honorable knight. Most men would have kept this gem for themselves. It's worth a fortune." He spun around, twirling in place. His tail slammed into the inn.

A tremor passed through the wall. The shutters loosened from their hinges, swinging precariously from the few nails that still held them in place.

Bruce held up his empty hands. "Please, if you could just calm down."

The dragon paused in his gaiety to look at Bruce. He held the crystal in one hand and the other flew to his mouth. His eyes grew wide and he gulped. Then his long neck lurched backward like a whip ready to strike. And then it did. The great head rushed at Bruce as flames shot from the dragon's mouth. Fire overtook the building beside him and several others nearby. His armor grew unbearably hot and it felt like his clothes were burning beneath the metal. He jumped up and down, attempting to find relief.

The dragon pounded on his chest with his fist a couple of times. "Sorry, I get gas when I'm excited." He cast a worried glance from side to side. "I, uh, I should probably be going. Thank you so much for finding my crystal."

Flames leapt up the wall behind Bruce, sizzling and snapping. Black smoke swirled through the air. He was not about to let this all end with nothing to show for all his trouble. Anger boiled inside him.

The dragon tucked the crystal under his arm and got up on his haunches.

Covered in sweat and coughing from all the smoke, Bruce drew his sword.

The dragon leapt into the air, only to slam back down to the ground on his clawed feet.

The burning wall of the inn shook. The cracks spread and widened. Shutters clanged to the street. The building to his left creaked and groaned. Wood on the building to his right snapped and sizzled.

Bruce slipped behind the dragon.

The dragon flapped its great wings, fanning the flames in the process.

Red hot embers flew upward, alighting on the thatched roof of the inn. It burst into flames. The wall of the building on the right collapsed, spilling chunks of wood and clay tiles into the street.

Bruce tripped on the bits of stone underfoot. The

dragon's wings kicked up a massive wind, swirling sparks into the smoke-filled air. He choked on the ashes and coughed until he inhaled a great mouthful of smoke. With his sword still in hand, he crept forward to the floundering dragon.

The dragon leapt upward again, gaining a bit of air before falling back to the street. Everything shook.

Bruce held his sword with both hands and raised it. The dragon never even looked over his shoulder to see the strike. That disappointed Bruce just a little. It was hard to make a stab in the back sound like a glorious battle, but with a quarter of the town on fire by now, there wasn't time to play this out like the tales of battle the teachers had spun at knight school. He sunk his sword into the dragon's side, right under its flapping wings.

The dragon did turn around then. It snapped at him with its long, sharp teeth, and then it coughed and tried to gain air once more. Six flaps later, it collapsed on its side, sending a tremor through the street.

Bruce fought to free his sword.

A terrifying creak filled the air. Bruce looked up just in time to see the wall of the inn tip forward. Flames rose from the sign bearing the smiling sheep. The sheep came closer and closer. The wall collapsed on top of him with a shattering crash.

🐉 Epilogue 🐉

Svetlana gazed up at the new sign. "What do you think, Daddy?"

"Knights Inn is a perfect name."

Svetlana beamed. "The sword-backed chairs should be in next week and Olga and Bjorn should have the chain-link curtains done in a few days. What about the plaque? Do you like it?"

Gildersnorf gazed down at the gilded wooden rectangle. "On this very spot, Bruce the Dragon Slayer defeated Jaskernect the scourge of Holden, and returned the legendary God's Eye to the hands of the Dwarves."

"Very nice, Svety. Bruce truly was a great and honorable knight." said her mother.

Her father patted Svetlana's shoulder. "Shame he didn't live to spend the reward for returning the God's Eye. After seeing the profits from the plans the two of you came up with for the sheep, I would have liked to have seen what he could have done with all that gold."

"I think he would have approved of how we spent the reward for him." Svetlana scanned the renovation progress reports for all of their inns. She couldn't wait until they were all complete. Everyone would know of Bruce's heroic acts.

"The weavers are just about finished with the first shipment of holy woolen socks. The sweaters and scarves should be here before winter," said Timbraelveayia. "Guess I'll have to stay out of the gift shop."

"I'm just happy you're able to be home again," said Svetlana.

Timbraelveayia wrapped her free arm around Svetlana to hug her. "With the sheep staying at the artist colony, you'll have to put up with my artistic whims here."

"I can deal with a little paint on the tables," said her father, nodding happily at the pile of painting supplies her mother had set up in the corner of the dining room, near the window that let in the morning light.

Her parents smiled at one another. Svetlana hadn't seen them so happy in years.

Her son let go of his grandmother's hand to put his tiny hand into her own. He smiled up at her with his big dark eyes.

Her father gazed down at the boy. "Are you

ready to tell me the truth about the boy's father yet, Svety? Bruce is a hero now, nothing for you to be embarrassed about."

Timbraelveayia sneezed.

The boy looked up at all of them. "MoOoommy?"

About the Author

Jean Davis lives in West Michigan with her musical husband, two attention-craving terriers and a small flock of chickens and ducks. When not ruining fictional lives from the comfort of her writing chair, she can be found devouring books and sushi, weeding her flower garden, or picking up hundreds of sticks while attempting to avoid the abundant snake population that also shares her yard. She writes an array of speculative fiction.

She is the author of *The Narvan* series and several standalone books including *A Broken Race, Sahmara, The Last God, Destiny Pills and Space Wizards,* and *Dreams of Stars and Lies.*

Read her blog, *Discarded Darlings*, and sign up for her mailing list at www.jeandavisauthor.com. You'll also find her on Facebook and Instagram @ JeanDavisAuthor, and on Goodreads and Amazon.

Made in the USA
Monee, IL
09 May 2021

67040941R00138